"Just What Are You Doing in Here?"

Dominic demanded angrily. "Can't you see that there are people out there waiting for you?"

Jennifer stood up, white with rage. She narrowed her eyes to meet his glowering look. "I am doing my job to the best of my ability, Mr. Martin," She retorted. "And if you are not satisfied, I am more than willing to leave. With suitable recompense, of course."

His blue eyes darkened until she felt as though she must drown in their deep pools. He stepped forward. "Perhaps you would consider this suitable recompense, Miss Evans?" he asked mockingly before his demanding lips met hers...

AUDREY BRENT
is an American writer currently living in California. She has travelled extensively here and abroad. She admits to particularly enjoying the mountains in all seasons. She has backpacked on lesser known wilderness trails in the Grand Canyon and plans to use more western landscapes in her future novels.

Dear Reader,

Silhouette Romances is an exciting new publishing series, dedicated to bringing you the very best in contemporary romantic fiction from the very finest writers. Our stories and our heroines will give you all you want from romantic fiction.

Also, *you* play an important part in our future plans for Silhouette Romances. We welcome any suggestions or comments on our books, which should be sent to the address below.

So enjoy this book and all the wonderful romances from Silhouette. They're for *you!*

Silhouette Books
Editorial Office
47 Bedford Square
LONDON
WC1B 3DP

AUDREY BRENT
Snowflakes in the Sun

Silhouette *Romance*

Published by Silhouette Books

Copyright © 1981 by Ann Boyle

First printing 1981

British Library C.I.P.

Brent, Audrey
    Snowflakes in the sun.
    I. Title
    813'.54   PS3552.R388

ISBN 0-340-27118-3

Printed and bound in Canada for
Hodder and Stoughton Paperbacks, a
division of Hodder and Stoughton Ltd.,
Mill Road, Dunton Green, Sevenoaks,
Kent (Editorial Office: 47 Bedford
Square, London, WC1 3DP)

Snowflakes
in the Sun

Chapter One

She had pursued her hopes and her dreams throughout with reasonable success until now. Surely she couldn't be defeated on this last step of her journey to a new job, a new life.

Jennifer drew in a deep breath of the crisp winter air and gave the great mountain a glare of defiance. Rainbow Ridge Ski Lodge must be up there somewhere, but Lookout Mountain rose so high that a cloud of bright mist and swirling snowflakes sparkled by unexpected sunlight completely hid its summit from her sight. She hadn't dreamed that the Sierra Nevada mountains would be so high, so rugged, or the chair lift that carried people up to it would appear so fragile.

Jennifer had been told that her size and strength were all concentrated in her spirit, which seemed too large, too strong to be housed within her small and delicately proportioned frame. Now as she looked up at the mountain and realized that she had to master it somehow, to get up to Rainbow Lodge, even her spirit seemed to have shrunk to miniature size.

This is ridiculous! she told herself as she silently fought down her fear. *I'll get up that mountain if I have to climb it on foot!*

She stood to the side of the lift's loading platform, out of the way of the surge of hurrying skiers eager to make full use of the brief winter daylight. None of them appeared to notice her reluctance to trust her safety to the swaying chairs. None of them appeared even to see Jennifer as they moved quickly past her and into position to let the chair scoop them up and move them smoothly, turning the line of them into a bright garland being carried up the steep face of the mountain.

Fear had played little or no part in Jennifer's life until now. Nothing in western Oklahoma where she had spent most of her twenty-three years had intimidated her, not the violent windstorms or the floods, not the droughts or the intense heat of summer, nor the animals that inhabited the vast open plains, not even the long years of caring for her invalid, bereaved father, confining though they had been.

Yet now, gazing up at the great mass of Lookout Mountain with its chairs that seemed to grow smaller and more fragile as they crept up the treacherous mountainside, she knew the acrid taste of fear.

But surely her employer . . . What was his name? Dominic Martin, that was it. Surely he would understand. The hotel management school that sent her to fill the unexpected mid-season vacancy must have explained to him that Jennifer was a stranger to the mountains. Since he had to have someone immediately, he couldn't be too selective and Jennifer knew her qualifications for the job were good. Once she made contact with Mr. Martin, everything would fall into place and her uneasiness would disappear.

Yet how could she ever overcome the obstacle of the mountain's steep face to reach him in his aerie?

The youth whose duty appeared to be seeing that each skier got safely into one of the double chairs noticed her at last. He said, "You waiting for somebody?"

Jennifer shook her head no, allowing the wind to catch a smoky streamer of her hair that escaped from the fur-trimmed hood of her green parka. She said, "Isn't there some other way I can get to Rainbow Ridge Ski Lodge?"

The boy's sun-bronzed brow crinkled into the creases of astonishment. "Good gosh, no. What'd you expect, a freeway up *this* hill?" He gestured toward the steep mountain face that rose behind him.

He was very young. She smiled at him and said, "I have to get up there."

He grinned in return. "That's what they all say. You flatlanders want fun the easy way."

"I'm not here for fun," Jennifer protested. "I was sent to replace . . .".

The startling effect her words had on him made her break off in mid-sentence. Not even his suntan could hide the color that mounted to his face. His eyes bulged with shock as he said, "You're Lodi's replacement? Good gosh! Lodi'll split her body cast if she finds out a flatlander's supposed to fill her boots."

"I was told I wouldn't have to ski."

He sighed. "Maybe for the job you don't have to ski, but what's the point in coming to a place like the Rainbow . . ." He broke off to give her an apologetic grin. "You see, Lodi's like me, a real dedicated skier. I admit I think flatlanders who come here dressed like you wouldn't believe, and never step into a binding are the pits, but . . ."

"You mean my ski suit isn't . . ." Jennifer glanced down at the green outfit, the bib pants with their matching, down-filled parka that she had hoped would give her confidence. Surely it couldn't be that wrong.

The youth's face twisted into a grimace. "Well, on you it looks great, but . . ." He stopped, then shrugged his shoulders, and like one tackling an unpleasant but necessary task, said, "These clothing stores'll sell you everything they can get you to buy, and they must have figured you out for a sucker."

"You mean this isn't what I should be wearing?"

He looked more and more uncomfortable, but he went on doggedly, "I just thought I'd better warn you instead of letting you walk into that pack of hounds like an unsuspecting rabbit and . . . Well, there's a lot of people who think the more they dress up the better they can ski."

Jennifer's laugh was rueful as she said, "I guess that's exactly the trap I fell into."

He shook his head. "If you've ever watched skiing on TV you know that super skiers dress for work, not for showing off their clothes." He grinned. "But you probably spent a bundle on that outfit."

"I did," she admitted. "More than I could afford."

"Like I said, on you it looks good. Really. Besides,

flatlanders make more money for ski resorts like they do for clothing stores. I shouldn't downgrade them . . . Hey, that line's bunching up behind you. These guys've paid for prime ski time, and I'd better see they get it. Mind waiting a few minutes?"

"I'll wait," Jennifer said, but she couldn't help being deflated. This job opportunity, coming even before she had finished the course in hotel management, meant a lot to her, the chance at last to broaden her horizon, to escape what had come to seem her monotonous background of endless flat plains and a small community. Lonely and restless since her invalid father's death, she wanted to find out something about the rest of the world. A glamorous ski resort had sounded like the ideal place to begin. She had considered herself more than fortunate that the school's head regarded her as the only possibility to fill the spot when the urgent appeal came for a mid-season replacement for an Activities Coordinator. Jennifer had been certain she could handle the job. Until she found herself surrounded by the mighty mountains.

But surely Dominic Martin would understand, she told herself. Surely the school had told him she was new to the mountains, a stranger to skiing. Dominic Martin would be patient, understanding, helpful, if only she could get up there to meet him.

She stood to one side watching as one skier after another came onto the platform and, as the attendant gave the word, slipped easily into place for the next upgoing chair. They all seemed to get on with no effort or worry. Surely she could do the same.

When the last of a group of passengers had been

started on the way up, the attendant turned back to her. "Have you met the guy who owns all of us?" he asked.

"Owns all . . . What do you mean?"

He grinned, brushing snowflakes from his eyelashes. "Dominic Martin, or course. He owns the place, he owns us."

Jennifer raised her chin. "Nobody owns me."

He gave her an exaggerated wink. "Then you haven't met him."

"No," she admitted. "Is he hard to work for?"

He frowned. "Depends. Come on. Let's get you started before that mob getting out of the van in the parking lot gets here."

He reached out to grasp her arm, but suddenly Jennifer drew back. "Don't bother with me. I can just hike on up the mountain."

"You can . . . what!" His voice croaked. "Now you've made my morning! Really! The Man would have my head if I let you do that! Don't you see how steep this face is?"

Jennifer hadn't been sure she really intended to hike up, so it was a relief to find she couldn't be allowed to. She said, "Well, let's get it over with. Show me how to mount this wild bronco."

His teeth flashed in a grin. "That's the spirit. I promise you this is one bronc that won't throw you." He reached for her suitcase. "First I'll move your luggage out of the way. I'll send it up later on the dummy."

Jennifer assumed he must mean some part of the lift designed to carry inanimate objects, but her luggage was the least of her worries now.

The attendant caught hold of her arm while he explained, "When I give you a little shove, you move over and stand on that square, see? Then bend over and let the chair come and scoop you up. That's all you have to do. It's simple."

His grin was meant to instill confidence in her, but it fell short of its purpose. She hadn't needed this much courage to mount her first skittish, bucking horse.

Nevertheless, she tried to follow his directions now. Drawing in a deep breath, she waited for his signal. When it came, she plunged toward the chairs.

"Easy!" he cried. "Don't rush it!"

His warning came too late; her boots slipped on a patch of ice. Jennifer struggled to regain her balance.

The attendant grabbed her and jerked her out of the way of the next oncoming chair.

Safe again, she clung with shaking legs to the young boy for support.

Even her voice shook when she spoke, although she managed to put laughter into it as she said, "Hey, you said it wouldn't throw me, but it tried hard enough." Then, more seriously, "Can't you stop the chair while I get on?"

"Can't I what? Oh God! What d'you think I am, Hercules?"

She laughed. "I didn't mean with your bare hands. Isn't there an emergency switch?"

"Yeah, but that's for emergencies! If I used it every time some flatlander turned chicken, I wouldn't keep my job long."

"You mean there are other people as bad as I am about getting onto the chair?"

"That's why I'm here, lady, that's why I'm here."

Knowing she wasn't the only uninitiated one made her feel better. She said, "All right, I'm ready for another try if you are."

"Not to worry. Here comes The Man himself. He'll take over."

Jennifer followed the young attendant's gaze as he tipped his head back to squint into the bright distance.

There could be no doubt as to the identity of the man approaching in the only occupied chair in the line of those coming down the mountain. Supreme confidence emanated from him like an aura. No one could doubt that Dominic Martin owned the mountain. Perhaps he did make some people feel as if he owned them too.

He'll never own me! Jennifer vowed silently.

Although from this distance she couldn't distinguish his features, his shock of red hair caught fire from the sun's light, defying the snow falling around him. He sat relaxed, his dark jacket carelessly open, as if daring the falling snowflakes to freeze upon him.

She gasped. He must not find her quavering with fear. Yet as the empty chairs glided smoothly past her bringing the one carrying him closer and closer, she found herself completely unable to move. In stunned fascination Jennifer watched him approach.

Dominic Martin sat easily in the lift chair. His proud head moved slowly from side to side as he surveyed the snowy country around him. When his chair reached the platform, he rose smoothly. As his boot touched the platform he stepped aside, out of the path of the moving line. His eyes swept quickly over Jennifer, but she had no doubt that he was aware of every feature, every flaw.

"I see you've got another . . . flatlander." His voice

was contemptuous. Jennifer's color mounted. To judge her so soon! What arrogance!

Before she could answer, Dominic Martin said, "I'll take her off your hands." As if she were a piece of luggage, unable to hear or speak up!

"I'll get onto the chair myself, thank you, if you'll move out of my way." She knew there were icicles in her voice, but she did not care. She took a step toward the line of chairs. Sudden anger fueled her courage; she no longer feared these moving metal monsters.

Her way was blocked by Dominic Martin's extended arm.

Before she could draw breath, he had caught her around the waist, lifting her up as he stepped into place in the line of upgoing chairs. He set her down on the far side of the benchlike seat and sat down beside her, reaching across her to fasten the bar over their laps.

Unable to catch her breath, Jennifer was temporarily speechless. The touch of his hands on her body had the effect of an electric shock, and her blood pounded in her ears.

Fighting for control of her emotions, she said, "You needn't have changed your plans for me."

"My visit to the village can wait. I stress safety at the Rainbow, and you novices tend to plunge in over your depth. You have to be shown that these mountains can be treacherous as well as beautiful." He turned his head and captured her with his stare, as if challenging her to doubt either the mountain's treacherousness or their beauty.

But the intense blue of his eyes was a distraction, and more time than Jennifer intended passed before she managed to say, "I'd have made it up eventually."

"Eventually isn't quick enough. You were holding up a line of skiers." His heavy brows bunched up, gathering snowflakes, as he frowned at her. "You don't seem to realize how dangerous . . ."

Unwilling to be treated like a child, Jennifer interrupted to say, "I wouldn't have fallen out of the chair."

Surprising her, he laughed, etching a brace of fine lines at the corners of his eyes. "You've a temper." He shrugged. "In any case, I won't allow you to ski before you take lessons. I can see you're too impulsive to be turned loose on my slopes without lessons. But you may choose between downhill and cross-country skiing. We have equipment and facilities for both at the Rainbow."

Jennifer could feel anger swelling within her, but before it could explode, he said, in a pleasantly conversational tone now, "Are your reservations for a lengthy stay at the Rainbow?"

"I . . . I'm not a guest. I've come to work here." She was afraid the wind had blown away her faint answer.

But Dominic Martin had not missed hearing. "You've what! *You* are Lodi's replacement?"

She studied her thickly gloved hands as her fingers twisted each other. "I'm the replacement for your Activities Coordinator." Then she looked up in defiance. "But I was told I didn't need to ski."

He turned away to look down on the jewel lake that lay far below them.

Jennifer's breath caught. *His eyes matched the rich blue of the lake.*

"Sapphire Lake," he said, jabbing his hand to show her. "Beautiful, isn't it?"

Sapphire eyes, her subconscious registered. Aloud she answered, "Yes."

As if he had not broken in to name the lake, he went on, "No, skiing isn't required of the Activities Coordinator. But you'll find it helps, especially in coping with the problems among your ski instructors."

"My ski instructors?"

His teeth flashed white in the sunlight. "The ski instructors are yours, all right. Your problem."

He explained that the schedule of classes and private lessons came under the Activities Coordinator's duties as did organizing entertainment for guests, including cross-country tours. "You'll be able to cope with the problems better if you speak the language. You'll take lessons." It was an order.

Her attention focused on her efforts to understand, she said, "What kind of problems are you talking about?"

He bent toward her, intent on his subject. "Those four instructors, three men and a woman, are expert skiers. They have unlimited energy and a certain amount of temperament. They get bored when life becomes too easy and they are stuck with too many beginners' classes without enough opportunity to stretch their muscles or use up their energy. And skiing is their life. You've got to keep them from cutting each other's throats, or someone else's. Even their harmless pranks can get out of hand now and then."

"People are people everywhere," Jennifer argued. "I doubt if their problems will be too different from those of a hotel staff." But something within her reminded her that she had had no experience as yet with handling even the problems of a hotel staff. Studying theories wasn't the same.

"Maybe they're no different," he said, holding her with his electric stare. "In any case, I hope you can handle this bunch."

Jennifer met his gaze steadily. "I can and I will."

He did not reply, but neither did he release her from his gaze, and Jennifer heard her heartbeat throbbing in her own ears. She could not deny his male magnetism. Perhaps that was part of her reason for wanting so intensely to hate him, to deny the effect of this magnetism.

She realized that Dominic Martin had begun speaking again, and that she had missed the first part of what he had said. She brought her attention sharply into focus as he said, ". . . safety rules."

"Safety rules?" she echoed.

His wide mouth twisted into a wry grin. "You weren't listening, were you." It wasn't a question.

"The . . . When the chair passes a tower it rattles so loud I . . . " She broke off as she realized that they hadn't passed a support tower for some time. Her excuse had been a poor choice.

"Yes," he agreed with a mocking grin. "There is a tower just ahead. I'll wait until we've passed it to repeat what you weren't able to hear."

She turned to face him directly. "All right, I wasn't listening. There's so much that's new here, I can't absorb everything at once and you've no right to expect me to."

One of his eyebrows jutted up toward the line of his fiery hair and his face hardened as he said, "I have every right to expect you to be competent in your job, and an important part of it is to enforce my safety rules."

Now her temper had taken fire to match the flame of his hair. "Then wouldn't it be more efficient if you wrote down those rules for everyone to read?"

"What do you call that?" His hand made a quick thrust to draw her attention to another of the printed signs planted in the snow under the chair lift. She had given them but scant attention as they passed. Even now she was distracted by the man himself. He wore no gloves! Was he invincible, insensitive to the biting cold, this mountain man whose face was all planes and hollows with dark shadows, like the mountains that surrounded him?

"Can you read it?" he persisted.

"Of course I can!" Like the others, the sign read, *Closed to skiers. Skiing forbidden.*

Jennifer swallowed the gravel that seemed stuck in her throat and tried to avoid the triumph in his eyes.

Dominic Martin said, "Perhaps you haven't noticed a succession of those signs. There is always some foolish skier, more often than not one of *your* ski instructors, who insists on defying even those signs. You are to see that they don't succeed."

If only his eyes weren't such an intense blue!

Jennifer blinked away the snowflakes and said, "You needn't worry. I'll do anything that is required of me. I'll learn your safety rules. You can stop treating me as though I were a brainless child."

His eyes narrowed. For an instant Jennifer thought he might resort to violence. But then, to her surprise, he laughed. "You've plenty of brains, it's your judgment I'm questioning. And as for treating you like a child, the way you spit at me, you're more cat than child. But right now if you value your safety, maybe even your life, you'd better obey me instantly. We're approaching the upper landing, and there's a trick to getting off this lift, especially in this fog."

He had scarcely spoken when their chair was swallowed up by the glittering, gray-white cloud.

"Lift your feet!" His command was terse. With no thought of questioning him, Jennifer followed his example by raising her feet until her legs were parallel with the seat of the chair.

With a quick thrust, Dominic Martin lifted the bar from over their laps, reached around Jennifer, and caught her waist with both his hands in a grip that had nothing of sentiment or sensuality in it.

As the platform of the upper deck gradually emerged from the gloom, she felt the tightening of his muscles as he picked her up.

"Feet down. Now!" he commanded.

She dared not disobey, and in an instant she found herself standing on the platform, safely out of the way of the moving chairs.

Now that she was safe on the platform, Jennifer grew annoyed, and she turned to ask him how he expected her to learn to ride the chair alone if he continued to lift her onto and off of it.

But she was interrupted. A young man dressed in outdoor clothing came up to Dominic Martin and said, "That cornice on the Skyline looks ready to go. Nick said you were on the way up and I waited. Can you come see about it?" He gave Jennifer an uneasy look as if he thought she might claim Dominic's attention.

Dominic's facial muscles tightened. "A bad avalanche year. You've closed the Skyline?"

The young man nodded.

Dominic turned to Jennifer. "I'll have to go. Cassie'll help you get settled. Go inside and see her."

Jennifer started to ask Dominic who Cassie might be and where she might be found, but he had already forgotten her. He and the younger man had left the platform and were striding off together across the snow. Heads bent close, their hands made sweeping gestures as they discussed the problem.

Well, Jennifer thought, this was only one more nearly impossible task Dominic Martin expected her to accomplish with little or no instruction or help. He had challenged her, and she had assured him she could and would do a competent job. Now it was up to her to prove the statement she had made with such confidence.

But her greatest challenge, Jennifer suspected, would be her relationship with the enigmatic and dynamic Dominic Martin himself.

Chapter Two

For a time Jennifer stood on the upper platform outside Rainbow Ridge Ski Lodge, staring into the mist-shrouded distance, while the falling flakes of snow tangled in her eyelashes. Although the sun did not penetrate the cloud that surrounded this part of the mountain, it turned the snowy landscape into a shimmering brightness that made her close her eyes against the glare.

But in the semidarkness behind her lids she saw the sharp outline of Dominic Martin's strong, masculine profile, the heavy brows shading those remarkable eyes, the Roman nose and the unyielding mouth. With an impatient flick of her head, Jennifer flung her eyelids open to find that the cloud had split apart revealing a patch of incredibly blue sky against which rose a jagged ridge of needlelike pinnacles too sharp to hold the snow. Caught now by the sun, they turned to rosy gold in the morning light.

Following these peaks across the horizon, her eyes rested on the sparkling white dome that must be Lookout Mountain's summit. Beautiful. Breathtakingly beautiful.

She shaded her eyes with her hand and squinted into the intense brightness. The slopes below this summit were sprinkled with dark trees in the midst of which rose another ski lift. Countless skiers skimmed over the lower slopes surrounding this lift. Distance robbed the figures of color so that they resembled insects crawling over snow.

The sound of laughter and shouting floated up to bring a smile to Jennifer's lips. This was a totally new experience for her, the new environment she had been seeking. Her imagination pictured her as one of those skiers, competent and graceful as she floated down the smoothly packed slope.

When into this picture the image of Dominic Martin came to join her as they sped down the slope, Jennifer wrenched her thoughts back to reality. She walked purposefully across the platform toward the building that must be the lodge to present herself for work. She would find this Cassie and get settled; perhaps she could even begin to organize her work before he returned. She would show Dominic Martin how efficient she was!

Before she could enter the lodge, a crowd of laughing skiers burst through the doorway, choking the opening so that Jennifer had to wait until all of them had spilled out.

They wore casual clothing that Jennifer would not

have considered warm enough for the snowy day, close fitting jerseys topped by sleeveless down-filled vests. Some even wore jeans, well tailored, but not what the clothing shop had recommended for skiing.

The most remarkable thing she noticed about the skiers was their headgear. Each one seemed to have outdone the other in choosing a brightly colored hat and decorating it with individuality. Fun hats, Jennifer thought, especially delighted by one with its crown turned into a clown face by brightly colored patches appliquéd onto it. She made up her mind to have a fun hat even though she might stick to her original choice of ski clothing. She would have a hat to express her own personality.

At last she was able to enter the large room that appeared to be the lounge. The room, crowded with people, was steamy with the odor of wet woolens. The beat of rock music from a loudspeaker vibrated into every corner, interrupted now and then by a mechanically amplified voice, high pitched or rasping, paging an individual or making an announcement to which no one seemed to listen.

Jennifer glanced around for some clue to help her find this Cassie person, and saw at the far end the high counter above which hung a sign, Reception. She headed for that. Surely here would be the place to get the information she sought.

As she threaded her way to the reception counter, everyone seemed to look straight through her, too intent on their own pursuits to give thought to an outsider. Jennifer felt very much an outsider. She wondered if the time would ever arrive when she would become part of this happy, carefree crowd of skiers.

Reminding herself that she had a job to do, she elbowed her way between groups of people.

When at last she reached the reception desk, she saw that here was one person who was aware of her existence.

The deeply suntanned, blond girl behind the desk filled her tee shirt more than adequately so that one could hardly escape seeing the large logo with its skier following the multihued curve of a rainbow. The girl's full lips turned down in a pout while her eyes made Jennifer think of blue-black steel. Jennifer had the feeling that those eyes had been appraising her as she managed the last distance to the desk, and that the girl not only knew where she had purchased her green outfit, but the exact amount she had paid for it.

I won't be intimidated by a snip of a girl receptionist, Jennifer told herself. She drew in a breath, raised her chin, and forced a smile as she came to the counter and rested her forearms on its high surface. "Hi, I'm . . ."

Jennifer got no further, for two young men came up to the counter, and the girl turned her attention to them as if Jennifer had vanished.

"Hi," she said to them. Now her full mouth turned up at the corners. "You guys have a fun plan in mind?"

"Yeah, Cassie," one of them said. "Ski the Starshoot with us this afternoon."

So this was Cassie who was supposed to help her, Jennifer mused.

Cassie nibbled the end of a pencil for a moment, then said, "Sounds great to me, Dave, but Dominic just bawled me out for taking too much time off last week."

"It's deep powder out there, Cassie," Dave said.

"Oh!" Cassie moaned. "You know how I love that beautiful stuff!"

"We're letting you in on it early because you're a good friend, Cassie. It'll soon be packed down."

The other added, "Can't you make those goo-goo eyes at The Man? You know. . . ." He burlesqued a flirtation that made Cassie burst into a fit of giggles.

"You told us you had him twisted around your finger, didn't you?"

Cassie grinned. "Sure. Okay, guys, it's a deal. I'll meet you at the top of the Starshoot, all right?"

When arrangements had been completed and the men had left, Cassie turned at last and as if she had just now noticed Jennifer said, "You wanted something?" Her voice was flat now, lacking either its earlier sweetness or interest.

"I'm Jennifer Evans, the new Activities Coordinator. . . ."

"Oh, no!" Under the tan Cassie paled a little. "You mean *you're* the one who did me out of that prize job?"

This was too absurd even to rouse Jennifer's temper. She said, managing a smile, "I never heard of you until . . . today." On a quick decision she had omitted mention of Dominic Martin. "I was told you could help me get settled."

Cassie drew herself up in a poor imitation of hauteur. "Nobody told me what to do with you. You'll just have to wait until *Mr*. Martin returns. He went to the village."

So, Jennifer thought, *she doesn't know everything that goes on.*

"Hey, wait a minute." Cassie leaned across the

counter toward Jennifer. Her smile was pleasant, but Jennifer had caught the crafty gleam that flickered in her eyes before Cassie masked it away. "If you're really all that eager to get started on your new job, I'll tell you what you can do while you're waiting. Something urgent just came up and I've got to leave. You can hold down this counter for a couple of hours while I take care of it. That'll really get you brownie points with The Man."

Jennifer just looked at her. *Something urgent, like skiing with the two men.* She forced down the angry retort that pressed at her lips and managed to say in a voice that was reasonably even, "Sorry, I can't do that. I don't even know my way around the lodge yet. I'd never be able to answer questions, and I'm sure I wouldn't be able to keep your registration book in the order you like."

Without waiting for Cassie's reaction, Jennifer turned and walked away, quickly losing herself in the press of people.

She had made an enemy of Cassie, she knew. But then, hadn't she been Cassie's enemy from the instant she was chosen for the job of Activities Coordinator?

Jennifer trembled with anger and her head had begun to ache. If only she could find a quiet place to sit and regain her composure.

There was no vacant chair in the teeming lounge, but she could see that although the bar was closed at this hour of the morning, its door was open and there were comfortable booths where she might sit and wait for Dominic Martin to return.

She made her way to the darkened area and entered,

blinking to allow her eyes to adjust to the abrupt change from the lounge with its wide expanse of windows.

As her eyes adjusted, she saw that the room was deserted. She slid gratefully into one of the booths, resting her elbows on the table and, setting her chin into her cupped hands, she closed her eyes.

"Hey, what have we here, a damsel in distress?"

The sound of the male voice made Jennifer open her eyes. A man approached her. When he came closer, his face brightened with recognition. "Didn't I see you out there?" A jerk of his head motioned back over his shoulder toward the main lounge.

Jennifer recognized him as one of the two men who had been trying to make the skiing date with Cassie at the reception counter. She nodded.

He eyed her. "Cassie gave you a bad time, didn't she? Look, don't take it to heart. That's just our Cassie. Nasty disposition. But we put up with her." He grinned.

He was no older than herself, Jennifer guessed, more slightly built than Dominic Martin. Oh, why did she have to compare him with that disturbing man? He had longish hair of a nondescript color that was neither brown nor blond. Friendliness, apparently, was his chief virtue, and Jennifer was grateful for that.

He said, "Maybe it's because of Cassie's skiing that we put up with her bad disposition and selfishness. Boy, that girl can ski!"

For the first time, Jennifer noted the insignia on the sleeve of this man's jacket. Above the rainbow logo were the words, Ski School.

"You're one of the ski instructors here?" Jennifer asked.

"Yes, ma'am," he said with mock formality. "Should I sign you up for lessons . . ." With a brief glance at her outfit, he added, ". . . in my beginner's class?"

Her clothing had given her away again, Jennifer thought with discomfort. But she said, "Thanks, but I'm here to work, not to play. I might as well introduce myself. I'm Jennifer Evans, the new Activities Coordinator."

He did not manage to keep the shock from his face as he said, "Hi, I'm Linc, head of the ski school. I guess we'll be rubbing shoulders a lot. Glad to have you aboard, Jennifer."

She thanked him as she shook hands, then rose to her feet. "You're the first friend I've made here, Linc, and I'd love to talk to you some more, but I only came in here to wait until Mr. Martin returns to get me started on my work."

"The Man," Linc said under his breath.

"What was that?" Jennifer had heard the phrase, but she hoped to tease some reaction out of Linc toward their employer, something to help her understand Dominic Martin.

"I just meant I'd better not keep you hanging around here," Linc replied, giving her no satisfaction whatsoever.

But at least she had found someone who was not hostile toward her. For that Jennifer was grateful.

Linc walked with her to the doorway of the bar, and for a moment they stood there together. "Look, Jennifer," he said. "Why don't you let me teach you to ski? You've got to have some fun while you're here. You know about all work and no play."

She turned her head to laugh with him, and he put a friendly arm across her shoulders. "That thing with Cassie gave you a warped picture of our life here at the Rainbow. We do have fun. You'll see." His fingers squeezed her shoulder gently to emphasize the words.

It wasn't only the encounter with Cassie that gave her a dismal picture of life at the Rainbow, Jennifer thought. After spending a half hour on the open chair lift with Dominic Martin, she wasn't certain he intended for her to have any fun here.

As they stood together in the doorway, Linc said, "Anything I can do for you, Jennifer, just let me know."

She looked up at him and made a quick decision. "There is something, Linc." She told him about the fun hats she had admired on the skiers. "Maybe some kind of silly hat would make me look less like somebody who doesn't belong here. Will you help me find a hat I can decorate?"

"Sure thing. It's as good as done." Again his fingers squeezed her shoulder. Then with a casual good-bye wave he swung away to cross the lounge, and Jennifer turned in the opposite direction.

She found her way blocked by a giant wearing an open jacket. Tipping her head to look up, she met eyes of a rich blue, now as cold as the ice on Sapphire Lake. Dominic Martin. Conflicting emotions seethed within her. No matter what the expression in his eyes, they always caught her as in a spell. Yet every encounter with him left her furiously angry.

"I see you weren't bored while you waited for me," he said sarcastically. "You knew Linc before you came here?"

"Of course not. I . . ."

"You two seemed to waste no time in getting acquainted."

Jennifer stifled a gasp. What was he implying? She said, "Linc was friendly!" She wanted to add, That's more than you have been! Only her status as his employee kept her silent.

"I could see that he was. Quite friendly." Then, with no change of expression, he went on, "I'll see you in my office in fifteen minutes." With long, purposeful strides he was gone before she had time to take in the meaning of his words.

When she did, she felt anger wash over her like a hot shower. Linc's arm around her had been nothing more than a friendly gesture! Besides, Linc wasn't the type that Jennifer could fall in love with anyway! And what right had Dominic Martin to object if he had been? She muttered to herself, "He may own the mountain, but he doesn't own me, nor ever will."

She had just fifteen minutes to compose herself and prepare to face the lion in his den. Now she understood why everyone called him The Man. Dominic Martin was like no one she had ever known, a man unto himself, special.

No! I won't think of him as special!

Jennifer turned her attention doggedly toward threading her way between the groups of people to the reception counter. As much as she dreaded confronting Cassie again, that was the best place to learn the location of Dominic Martin's office.

As might have been expected, Cassie did not let her off with a simple answer to her question.

Cassie's grin did not match the expression of her eyes when she said, "I see you've made friends with Linc."

Had everyone in the lounge witnessed their appearing together in the bar's doorway?

Cassie twisted the knife still further. "I wouldn't have guessed you're the type for Linc, since you obviously don't ski." Her glance raked Jennifer as if to tear the handsome outfit from her shoulders.

"At least Linc is friendly," Jennifer replied, careful to keep her voice level.

"So I could see," Cassie said and giggled. Again Jennifer's remark had been turned into something other than what it was meant to be.

There was nothing to be gained by sparring with Cassie, Jennifer decided. She said, "Would you please tell me where Mr. Martin's office is?"

"He's calling you on the carpet, huh?"

"Someone has to tell me where to start work here," Jennifer said.

A door to the side of the reception desk opened and then Dominic Martin emerged. "Cassie, I am ready to talk to Jennifer now."

"Oh, sure, Mr. Martin," Cassie trilled. "I was just *trying* to explain to her where your office is." Her voice was saccharine, but her words made Jennifer appear too dense to follow directions.

Dominic Martin turned back into his office, leaving the door open for Jennifer.

As Jennifer started away from the reception counter, Cassie bent across it and in a whisper as venomous as a snake's tongue, said, "You swiped my job, now leave my man alone!"

"Your man?"

"Him." Cassie jerked her head toward Dominic Martin's office.

"You're welcome to him," Jennifer replied, wondering belatedly if she had made her voice ring with enough sincerity.

Head held high, she approached the open door of Dominic Martin's office.

He was working over some papers on a massive desk when she entered. He did not look up as she came to stand in front of his desk.

Although Jennifer told herself she had no interest in Dominic Martin as a man, only as her employer, she could not resist studying him as she waited for him to finish whatever held his attention.

Even without the bulk of a down-filled jacket, his shoulders appeared massive, stretching the cloth of his shirt. Defying the popular choice of turtleneck sweaters or jerseys she had seen here, Dominic Martin wore an open-throated shirt. Its blue matched that of his eyes. The light that came in through the window behind him had toned down the flame of his hair giving it the sheen of burnished copper, matched by the mat of curls spilling out of the shirt's opening and bristling along his forearms to his rolled up sleeves.

Jennifer saw the glint of a gold chain with a medallion, the gold no brighter than the copper of the hair that half hid it on his chest.

"You may close the door behind you."

Turning to do so, she took a moment to glance

around the room, hoping to glean a few clues to the man's personality from the appointments of his private office.

The desk, of course, dominated the room. Of highly polished dark wood, it was neatly stacked with papers. There was a single photograph, but its back was turned so that she saw nothing but the reverse of the frame. A telephone, impersonal and unrevealing, gave her no clues.

But the shelves of books looked as if they would be a gold mine of information about his tastes, if only she had time to study their titles. Several pairs of skis stood in a corner of the room, and a strange looking crisscross of leather straps that could be a harness hung nearby. Jennifer had to suppress a nervous giggle at the wildly absurd picture it stirred in her mind of Dominic Martin driving his employees, strapped into their harnesses, before him.

As she returned to his desk, Dominic Martin looked up and with a sweep of his hand indicated the chair across the desk from him. "You may sit down."

His casual permission annoyed her, and she said, "I prefer to stand."

With a shrug of his shoulders he rose from his chair and came around the desk to join her. But instead of standing beside her, he half sat on the edge of the desk, swinging his leg across its corner. With his arms folded across his chest, and his head tilted slightly to one side, he looked at her in silence for a long moment.

Jennifer waited, wondering if he would upbraid her for her refusal to comply with Cassie's unreasonable request to take over the reception desk. Or perhaps he would reprimand her for going into the deserted bar where Linc had followed her. Would Dominic Martin even give her the opportunity to explain that she had gone in alone and that Linc had come in later? Already he had misinterpreted Linc's friendly gesture, his arm across her shoulders.

Jennifer hoped that the anger in her fighting against the aura of his masculine strength did not show in her face. She braced herself for whichever misinterpretation Dominic Martin would choose to use against her.

But when at last he spoke, it was on neither of the subjects Jennifer had anticipated. Yet it startled her more.

Without releasing her eyes from his, he rose from his position on the desk and came to stand close to her. *Too close,* Jennifer thought, for she could feel his magnetism even before he raised his hands and rested them on her shoulders.

His fingers massaged the flesh of her shoulders while his eyes seemed to probe deep into her soul. "Jennifer," he said. "Are you afraid of me?"

"Of course not!" She spoke quickly, but she could hear the tremor in her own voice, not from fear but from an emotion she could neither define nor deny.

He smiled. It was the kind of smile she had not seen on his lips before, and it softened his hard masculine features.

"Then why are you so tense, my dear?" he persisted. "Why don't you relax with me?"

"How can I relax when you treat me as if I have no sense, or as if I were a child you're trying to train?" she stormed.

His brow lifted in surprise. A little flame of triumph flickered within her.

He said, "But I have to train you. You're new to this job, new to skiing, and even though we stress informality here, there are rules that must be followed. Of course, if you can't take . . ."

"I can't take the way you treat me!" Jennifer wrenched herself free of his grasp. "The way you laugh at me!" She spun around and strode across the room toward the two closed doors.

From behind her his quiet voice was almost gentle. "I didn't think you were a quitter."

His calm challenge added fuel to the flame of her temper. "You're . . . impossible!" She wrenched open the nearest door and started to cross the threshold.

With a gasp she stopped short. The room she had been about to enter was obviously Dominic Martin's bedroom, a very masculine bedroom, decorated in colors and designs as strong and bold as the man himself, bright orange mellowed by browns and rust.

Quickly, she closed the door. She heard no emotion in his voice when from behind her he said, "It's the other door you want."

Jennifer's anger drained away. Slowly she turned around to face Dominic Martin. "You're not laughing at me? Not angry?"

"Why should I be? For making a mistake between two identical doors! Now, Jennifer, I want you to go to your room and get settled."

"How can I? I don't know where my room is."

"Didn't Cassie show you where you're to stay?"

Surely he must know what kind of person Cassie was! But from his expression she guessed that he did not.

Now was her chance to get even with Cassie. She

could tell Dominic Martin just how hateful Cassie had been.

But that would be playing the same game that Cassie played, and Jennifer knew she could never live in peace with herself if she stooped so low. Surely Cassie would sooner or later betray herself to him. Meanwhile, Jennifer would simply have to stay aloof. With a great amount of restraint she said simply, "No."

"No doubt she was busy. I'll take you there myself. Come."

Pleased with the results of her forbearance, Jennifer left the office with Dominic Martin.

As he closed the door behind them, Jennifer heard from outside yelping and howling. Were there wolves in this country?

She tilted her head to look up at Dominic Martin, intending to question him. He was grinning.

"My dogs are calling me," he said. "They're impatient for a run over the snow." He explained that he had a team of matched Siberian Huskies he had trained to the dogsled. His eyes glowed with love and pride. "They count on their daily exercise and take pleasure in the romp." He went back to his office and returned with the harness Jennifer had noticed earlier.

He suggested that she might like to delay their errand in order to see the dogs and she agreed, her curiosity stirred. "I'd like to see them," she said.

Now Jennifer's seesaw feelings toward Dominic Martin took a sharp upward turn. Much of her earlier anger seeped away as she walked beside him down the corridor.

As they made their way along he explained why

Huskies are ideal for pulling a sled over the snow. "In addition to a marvelous chest," he said, "the Siberian Husky has a paw that's larger than most dogs' and well adapted to staying on top of deep snow."

Before she could ask any questions about the dogs or the sport, he had switched to another subject, apparently even more important to him than his dogs, running the resort.

"You know," he said, "we get all kinds of people at the Rainbow, from families with children to single young people seeking their own kind. All have one thing in common, however. They're on vacation; they've come here to relax and have fun. We have to provide something for everyone. We must have many different kinds of entertainment as well as skiing, to add to their enjoyment and fill their time. And I insist on providing an atmosphere of informality, bounded of course by the safety rules. I hope you will cooperate with this plan, Jennifer."

"Of course."

Without breaking his long stride, he said, "I want you to make an outline, a plan for a tentative program to be worked around the skiing lessons. I'm sure there are some of the ones Lodi used around. You can study these to see what sort of things the guests like to do. But you will of course improve on Lodi's plans. Cassie will give you whatever Lodi left."

Not if she can avoid it! Jennifer thought but did not say as she walked beside him, trying to keep up with his long steps.

As they crossed an intersecting corridor Cassie joined them, falling into step on Dominic Martin's other side, opposite Jennifer.

Ignoring Jennifer, Cassie cocked her head to smile up at him as she said, "I heard the dogs calling you, Dominic, and I just couldn't wait to see them again."

He said, "I'm taking Jennifer out to meet them. You may come along, Cassie, if there's someone covering the reception desk."

"Of course!" Cassie's look of hurt over an unjust accusation sent an itch of irritation along Jennifer's spine. "You didn't think I'd leave it unattended, did you?" Without giving him time to reply, she went on, "It's my break time, and Dave came along with no classes to teach until this afternoon. He practically begged to take over for me."

Dominic did not reply to this. His rugged masculine profile told Jennifer nothing of his reaction.

At last they came outside to the fenced area where the handsome dogs were kept. Jennifer was impressed by the intelligent and interestingly marked faces of the dogs. Their heavy coats mingled black, gray and white. Although the dogs were not unfriendly, their excitement made plain that their chief interest was in getting out for a run in the snow.

Cassie wheedled, "Dominic, you keep saying you'll give me a ride on the sled. Why can't you do it now? Please . . ." She drew out the word.

"Now is as good a time as any," Dominic answered. "Jennifer's got plenty to do while we're gone. Matter of fact, I see the ski shop's open now. I'll take her there and introduce her to the kids. They can fix her up with skis and boots."

He turned to Jennifer and added, "Maybe one of the instructors will be free to help you get the feel of the boards, Jennifer."

Behind them, the dogs' yelping and impatient howls drowned out whatever Dominic Martin called back to them. Jennifer saw the smug triumph that brightened Cassie's face.

Why couldn't Dominic understand what this transparent girl was doing, Jennifer thought, and hated him for not seeing Cassie through her eyes.

Chapter Three

Jennifer found the people in the ski shop pleasant but she sensed their disdain for her lack of skiing know-how. She felt keenly the sharp contrast between her sophisticated ski outfit and her complete ignorance of skiing.

Before the proper skis had been found for her, Linc came in with the other ski instructors. Each was properly introduced to Jennifer, and she had the feeling that she was being judged. She hoped she passed the test, for she remembered Dominic Martin's warning that she would be in charge of them and the job would not be easy.

Jennifer tried to appeal to the ski instructors when she said, with her best smile, "Even though I'm not a skier, I'm willing to learn. In fact, I think we're going to get along just fine if we all pull together like Mr.

Martin's dogsled team. I'll do the best I can, but I'll need your help. Okay?"

There was a tense moment's hesitation, and then Linc said, "Come on, gang. The Man's turned her skiing instruction over to us. It's up to us to teach Jennifer to ski well enough to make her outfit believable."

One by one, they broke into grins, extending their hands to shake. Jennifer relaxed in the realization that she had passed the first hurdle.

But for the next hour there was little chance for further relaxation. Linc had decided to start her out on cross-country skiing. He took her to a relatively flat stretch of snow to help her become accustomed to balancing on the long narrow boards. He explained to her the kick-glide and pole thrusting rhythm peculiar to that type of skiing.

It was hard physical work. Before long Jennifer found her layers of clothing much too warm. Now she understood the reason for the lightweight clothing the guests wore for skiing.

When she spoke of this to Linc, he said, "Jeans are okay for working out near the lodge in weather no colder than this, that is if you don't mind getting damp when you fall down in the snow." To venture farther from base, he warned, would be foolish without at least carrying along warmer garments.

It was near the end of the hour. Fatigue had turned Jennifer's muscles to rubber. As if to illustrate his words about falling into the snow, she lost her balance and toppled over into a drift.

When she tried to push herself up, she found herself too exhausted to do so.

Linc came to her rescue, lifting her to her feet. He continued to hold his arms around her, waiting until she could regain her balance.

"Is this how you give a ski lesson, Linc?" It was Dominic Martin's voice, and to Jennifer it seemed to carry the threat of a thunderbolt announcing the approach of a storm.

Immediately, Linc released his hold on Jennifer.

Without the steadying force of Linc's arms, Jennifer toppled once more into the snow.

Instantly, Dominic Martin was at her side, lifting her upright again. "You okay?" he asked without releasing her.

Why shouldn't I be? She wanted to shout, but the words somehow refused to come out. Linc's supporting arms had caused none of the electric shock that now raced through her as Dominic grasped her. Tears gathered behind her eyes and nearly choked her. "Yes, I'm all right," she finally stammered, hoping he would release her physically as well as from her conflicted emotions.

When he did remove his hands, Jennifer's legs would not support her. Once more she crumpled to a heap in the snow.

Linc said, "I didn't do anything. Honest. I was just helping her up when . . ." He broke off as Dominic Martin gave him a look that seemed to crackle with fire enough to melt the snow.

Dominic bent over Jennifer. The expression on his face might have been concern, but she was too angry to analyze it.

Instead, she glared up at him and said, "Even if we had been doing what you obviously assume, it's none of

43

your business. . . ." She squeezed her eyes tightly shut to hold back the tears that threatened to betray her by spilling from her eyes and trembling in her voice. They were tears of anger and exhaustion, but he would, of course, assume they showed weakness in her.

He said to Linc, as if Jennifer could not hear, "She tried to do too much in her first day. Not used to the altitude at that."

Jennifer's tears vanished instantly. Her eyelids sprang open and she shot him a murderous look. After all, it was he who had demanded all this of her in her first day, and only now had he shown any concern over her adjustment to the high altitude.

Before she could answer him as angrily as he deserved, he had gathered her up in his arms as if she were a child. She was being carried back toward the lodge by The Man himself, Dominic Martin.

Should she pound him with her fists? But her muscles refused to obey her commands. Instead, she relaxed into the comfort of his masculine strength. She could feel the steady pounding of his heart as her face rested against his broad chest, even smell the faint scent of his aftershave lotion. It smelled of lemon, tart and fresh, and of the outdoors.

Jennifer shifted her arms to a more comfortable position. As if of their own volition, they stole up around his neck as she sank into a dreamy state of lethargy.

He carried her into the room that was to be hers, and deposited her on the bed, standing beside her to look down at her. "Now," he said, "take a nap. You don't need any more exercise today. Later this afternoon will be time enough to work up those programs I told you I want outlined."

Being dumped so unceremoniously onto the bed fired Jennifer's anger again. She began, "Why don't you get . . . ?"

"By tomorrow you'll be used to the altitude," he said. It was as well that he interrupted her, for she had been ready to make a sarcastic suggestion that he get Cassie to do the plans.

Then he went on, "Tomorrow you'll have to start lessons in downhill skiing."

"Downhill! But I haven't learned enough about cross-country skiing yet!"

As if she hadn't spoken, Dominic said, ". . . a waste of everybody's time, Linc coaching you on cross-country. You could have learned as much by yourself as he taught you today." He stopped, drawing his brows together in a scowl so fierce that Jennifer dared not interrupt. Then with a jerk of his head he said, "All right, I'll take you out on the slope tomorrow myself." He bit off the words as if he were angry. *Probably he blamed her for wasting Linc's valuable time*, Jennifer thought.

I didn't ask for the lesson today, and as for tomorrow, you needn't bother," she said tartly.

He caught her eyes with his own piercing glance. "What's the matter, Jennifer, can't you take it?"

"Of course I can take it. But I must say, Mr. Martin, you expect a lot of your employees!"

Dominic's unexpected grin mocked her. "No more than they are capable of." He swung around and left the room.

"Blast that man!" Jennifer muttered, "he always seems to have the last word."

She did not sleep well that night. The thought of tomorrow's lesson in downhill skiing from Dominic Martin brought such a mixture of emotions that sleep eluded her. She was certain he would push her beyond her strength and ability and that angry words would pass between them.

"But I won't let him intimidate me," she whispered into the darkness. "And I won't do anything I don't feel like doing."

When the lesson began next day, however, Jennifer was astonished to discover that Dominic was a patient and thorough teacher. And rather than pushing her beyond what she wanted to do, he encouraged and inspired her to go beyond what she would have thought possible. More than that, he had an unsuspected sense of humor, laughing with her but never at her, when she fell awkwardly or made foolish mistakes.

Under his coaching Jennifer advanced quickly to the intermediate slope. She was so favorably impressed with his teaching that she said, "You must have had a lot of experience as a ski instructor, Mr. Martin."

His grin was crooked as he looked at her and said, "I've had a lot of experience in many things. . . . At one time or another, I have had to fill in on most of the jobs here at the Rainbow. But as long as we're going to be so closely associated, Jennifer, don't you think calling me Mr. Martin is a bit formal?"

Jennifer hesitated. She thought, *No matter what I call*

him, I'll never speak of him as The Man the way the others do.

He said, "My name is Dominic."

As if she weren't all too aware of that. Aloud she said, "All right, if you want, it's Dominic." She forced herself to add with what she hoped was a casual air, "Now, shall I try that turn once more?" Without waiting for his reply, she dug her poles into the snow and started down again.

The day was bright with the sun threading in and out among the fleecy white clouds. As they rode the lift up beside the intermediate slope, a shower of snowflakes descended upon them. For a few minutes the snowfall was so thick and fast that it all but blinded Jennifer. She wished that she had worn protective glasses. The flakes caught in her eyelashes as she released the poma at the top and glided to a halt, groping her way through a blur of melting snow.

Dominic, who had come up directly behind her, caught her arm and guided her with his hand on her arm until she was safely out of the way of other skiers approaching on the lift.

As they stood together, Dominic pulled off his glove and gently brushed the flakes from her eyes. Then, grinning down at her, he said, "If that button you use for a nose were any more uptilted, lady, you'd be in danger of drowning. There's a snowflake on the tip that's ready to melt and run down now."

To her surprise, he bent down and licked the snowflake off, then brushed his lips across the tip of her nose in the lightest of kisses.

Astonishment made Jennifer jerk her head away,

and in that instant Dominic's expression clouded. He said, "That's enough ski lesson for today. You can get back to the lodge on your own. Work on those activities plans. I want them on my desk before the day is over." His voice was harsh as he swung abruptly away and skied off in the opposite direction.

For a few minutes Jennifer stood where she was, too astonished to move. She had been startled by the unexpected kiss, light and brief though it had been.

Then she began to feel annoyed. Dominic had said he'd had a lot of experience in many things. Maybe he wasn't referring only to the different jobs at the resort. His actions seemed to indicate plenty of experience in dealing with women, in manipulating their emotions. Maybe that was the experience he had referred to.

Why should I care how much experience he's had with women? Jennifer asked herself. Rather than forming an answer, she swung around on her skis and charged down the slope as fast as she could go.

During the next days, Dominic did not again offer to give Jennifer ski lessons. Yet often while she was skiing she heard the excited howling of his sled dogs or caught a glimpse of his fiery head, like a meteor moving across the snow, as he rode the runners of his sled. In spite of herself, she would find the blood coursing through her veins with an excitement she could not define.

Linc lived up to his promise to find a fun hat for her. One day when she returned to the lodge after skiing a trail with a group led by one of the other instructors, Linc presented her with the hat and a speech.

"It's your reward for being such a model student for our ski school," he proclaimed, and handed her a frothy concoction of bright pink-and-white polka dots and lace with a wide, floppy brim. "It's yours to decorate as you choose."

"It's perfect, Linc!" Jennifer cried. "Tomorrow's my day off and I'll wear it down to the village. I'll find something there to help me decorate it in the style it deserves."

She had wanted to visit the colorful village below the big chair lift, and now she had a reason to do so. This was a perfect way to celebrate her first week at her job.

So far it had been successful. At least, her plans for the guests' entertainment seemed to meet with Dominic's approval, for he had made no change in them. She had even begun to enter into the spirit of relaxed fun that pervaded the lodge. When she introduced a new game for some group's evening entertainment, she usually joined in playing it. Although Dominic Martin did not participate, he often strolled among the guests in the evening, or stood in the shadows at the edge of the room to watch. Jennifer could always sense his presence even before she caught sight of him, leaning casually against the wall, arms folded across his chest. But by now she had learned to mask the stirring of emotions the sight of him caused in her.

Linc was pleased with her progress in skiing now. However, Dominic seemed to be conspicuously absent whenever Jennifer appeared on the slopes. She reminded herself that she didn't care, except that she would have enjoyed showing him that she wasn't as incompetent as he seemed to think she was. On the whole, life at the Rainbow appeared to be running smoothly.

To add further to her sense of well-being this morning as she stepped onto the chair lift's loading platform, the sun glowed in a cloudless sky. Although there was a light wind, the air was warm. Jennifer had left behind her heavy down-filled jacket. Instead she wore a wool cardigan sweater under a lighter weight windbreaker and, of course, her pink hat. Dressed this way, she felt very much the seasoned skier.

She shared a downgoing chair with one of the maintenance crew. She had seen him often and found him likable. He told her he was on his way down to see his girl friend who didn't ski. They chatted about the girl friend, but Jennifer's thoughts drifted idly and fastened at last on the lovely view of Sapphire Lake sparkling in the sunlight.

In spite of herself, she wondered what Dominic was doing right now. Was he out with his dogsled and team on this fine day?

She gave her head a little shake to rid it of thoughts of the disturbing Dominic Martin.

The quick motion coincided with a sudden gust of wind. Jennifer's pink hat was caught by it and whipped from her head. Before her hands could grasp it, the hat had been swept down to wedge itself at a rakish angle on the corner of one of the *no skiing* signs far below the chair.

"Oh!" Jennifer cried. She bent far forward in her effort to see her hat as their chair moved away from it. Her seatmate reached out to grab her shoulders.

"Hey!" he cried. "You can't go after it!"

"But it's my new hat! Linc gave it to me!"

"You were going to fall out!" he scolded. "The village has a million crazy hats. You'll find another one."

Jennifer shook her head. "It wouldn't be the same. But thanks for the thought."

"Well, don't let it spoil your day." He gave her an encouraging grin. "You'll have fun in the village. Going to meet some guy there, I'll bet."

Jennifer shook her head. "No. Just going to shop." But suddenly she wished she were meeting Dominic Martin there to have the fun her companion on the chair had suggested. But of course, she thought wistfully, that could never be.

Chapter Four

The village was a colorful reproduction of an old-world community, with its buildings in the style of Swiss chalets. The bright sunlight turned painted flowers decorating carved balconies into cheerfully blooming spring gardens that seemed to defy the cold and to laugh at the snowbanks flanking the main street.

At first Jennifer merely strolled down the street, pausing to study the display windows of each shop. Most of these shops specialized in one line of merchandise, some showing skis and ski equipment while others displayed clothing suitable for skiing or after-ski relaxing. There was a bakery exuding the enticing aroma of warm, fresh-baked bread. Jennifer hurried past this temptation, for she wanted to get an overall picture of the village before she spent more than a few minutes of her valuable free day on one shop.

A florist window carried a variety of handsome and attractive arrangements, some so exotic that Jennifer suspected they must be artificial. But they looked so natural she could not differentiate between the real and the artificial.

She walked up one side of the street and down another, and at last allowed herself to step into a clothing shop where she tried on a beautiful long skirt of a soft woolen material that was a swirl of brilliant colors. It was warm and informal, and she thought it would be ideal for evenings spent in the lodge.

She debated about buying it. It would take a large bite out of her first week's salary, and she was not certain she had a blouse or top to go with it. Should she be sensible or celebrate her good fortune in getting this job?

Then she remembered the pink hat that had been blown from her head on the way down. The loss of that hat had been more painful than just the loss of an ordinary head covering. Linc must have understood her feelings when he found the hat for her, for it had raised her self-esteem immeasurably. She felt its loss keenly now.

She would have to replace the hat, even if she couldn't find one exactly like it. She must have a frivolous, silly hat before she could even think of buying anything else.

The saleswoman was looking at her expectantly as Jennifer pirouetted before the full length mirror. "You'll take the skirt? It's perfect for you, you know."

Jennifer sighed. "I know, and I love it. But there's something else I have to buy first, and I'm not at all certain how much I'll have to spend on that. I'll just have to delay buying the skirt."

"We could put it on layaway."

Jennifer shook her head. "No. By the time I could finish paying for it, it might be too late. Thanks, but I'll just take my chances and hope the skirt's still here when I'm ready to buy it."

She hurried to the dressing room to remove the skirt before further temptation overcame her.

When she came out of the shop, she tried to remember just where she had seen the store that now seemed a good possibility for finding the kind of hat she sought. It was in the far end of the village, she thought, and she hurried there now.

She was about to enter the store when she heard her name called, and turning to glance back over her shoulder, she saw Linc hurrying toward her. "Hey, wait up, Jennifer," he called as he came. "I brought you something special."

One of his hands was held behind his back, but when he reached her he whipped it out and said, "I guess you lost this on the way down, didn't you?"

In his hand he held the pink hat.

"Linc! How did you get it back?" Jennifer cried, reaching for the hat.

"Well, it's for sure you didn't give it to me. You didn't mean to throw it away, I hope."

"Of course not! It means so much to me!" She clutched the hat to her breast, grinning at him. "I just don't understand how you could possibly get it. The face of the mountain is . . ." She caught her breath as she remembered the *no skiing* signs Dominic Martin had pointed out to her, and how he had emphasized that they were to be enforced by Jennifer. "Linc! You didn't . . ."

Linc would not allow her to continue, however, nor, apparently, did he intend to explain how he had obtained the hat. Instead, he caught her arm and said, "Let's go celebrate the return of the hat. I know a good place." He hurried her along so fast that Jennifer had to stretch her legs to keep up with his longer ones. As they dodged around groups of people and singles walking along the narrow sidewalk, Jennifer was unable to discuss the return of the hat with him.

By now the sun was heading into a bank of clouds piled as white and as high as snowbanks. Jennifer's worry over how Linc had retrieved her hat dimmed the sunshine of her happiness just as the sunshine of the outdoors had been dimmed.

But the restaurant Linc took her to was warm and cheerful with brightly upholstered booths to offset the mellow, dim indoor lighting, and in no time she was able to shake off the feeling of apprehension.

The booths circled a scrap of a dance floor, and a coin operated tape deck sent forth music loud enough to drown out all depressing thoughts as well as most conversation.

After ordering coffee, they danced. Linc was a good dancer, Jennifer discovered, light on his feet and supple.

When at last they stopped dancing for a few minutes, they found their coffee had cooled to a tepid mediocrity.

Jennifer glanced at her watch and laughed. "I'd no idea so much time had passed, Linc. It's almost noon. I'll treat you to a lunch as a reward for rescuing my hat."

Her fingers gently smoothed the brim of the hat that lay on the banquette beside her.

"That's a deal," Linc said. "But I'll warn you I'm hungry, and this place has super tacos. I recommend them."

Jennifer preferred a hamburger, and Linc gave his order for two tacos along with her hamburger. While they waited for their food, they returned to the dance floor.

When the waitress brought their meal to the table, she said, "You people from the Rainbow?"

Both Linc and Jennifer nodded, expecting a discussion of the lodge or possibly of working conditions there.

Instead, the waitress said, "The Man sent word down for all personnel to return immediately. A storm's on the way."

Jennifer turned anxiously to Linc, but he only laughed. "If The Man thinks I'm going to let this free bread go to waste just because he's nervous about the weather, he's crazy." He sniffed appreciatively into the steam rising from his plate, and then picked up one of the tacos and crunched into it. "Mmm. Up to their usual standards," he mumbled over the mouthful.

"But, Linc," Jennifer protested. "Dominic's our employer."

Linc's eyes narrowed as he looked at her. Without putting down the taco, he said, "He doesn't own me. Does he own you, Jennifer?"

"Of course not! But . . ." But she worried.

"Then be quiet and eat your hamburger before it gets cold."

Jennifer had lost her appetite, and she only nibbled at her food. But Linc's appetite was not affected. When the tacos were gone, he ordered an enchilada and two glasses of wine. "The wine's on me," he said. "Maybe it'll help you not to worry."

His prediction came true. The warmth of the restaurant, the enticing music and Linc's reassurance made her forget her worries.

When Linc's appetite had been appeased, he summoned the waitress, but instead of asking for the check, he ordered another round of wine.

"Linc," Jennifer said. "We really have to get back."

"I said I'd pay for the wine."

"It isn't that, Linc. But we're defying Dominic's order to return. You know what a temper he has. It could cost us our jobs."

Linc shrugged. "Time The Man learned to curb his temper."

"But don't you see . . . ." Jennifer began.

He cut her off, making a face as he said, "Aw, sweetheart, you worry too much. How could The Man replace us this far into the season? Besides, that storm won't break until midnight at the earliest. The Man sees a couple of stray flakes of snow, he panics."

Jennifer could not imagine Dominic Martin in a panic. He was too strong, too sure. But the urgency of his message did seem a little absurd in view of the bright sunlight of this morning. She sighed and agreed to wait until Linc had finished his glass of wine.

He made no attempt to finish it, however, leaving his half-empty glass on the table opposite hers that had scarcely been touched. Instead, he rose to his feet and caught her hand. "One more dance to settle all that food before we go out to brave the cold, cruel world and The Man." There was mockery in his voice.

He did not wait for her consent, but drew her onto the floor as the machine blared out its music.

When the number ended Jennifer drew back from Linc. "Now," she said. "I don't care what you're going to do. I'm going back to the Rainbow the way Dominic wants us to."

Linc's eyes raked her. There was a mixture of teasing and mockery in his look that annoyed Jennifer as he said, childishly, "Scaredy-cat."

Jennifer caught his hand and laughed up at him, ignoring the irritation they both felt. "Oh, Linc, don't be absurd."

Something caused her heart to stop beating for an instant and she glanced beyond Linc to where the doorway had just been darkened by an ominous bulk. Instantly, Jennifer recognized Dominic Martin. She could tell by the way he stormed into the restaurant that he was furious.

She guiltily dropped Linc's hand as if it had burned her, feeling as though she had been caught in an illicit relationship.

"So there you are, Jennifer!" Dominic Martin thundered. The sound of his voice dominating the strains of music caused all heads to turn. "Didn't you get my message?"

Jacket swinging open, snowflakes frosting his shoulders and fiery hair, he strode across the dance floor to where they stood beside their table. Dancers scattered before him as dry powder snowflakes scatter before a sweeping wind.

When Dominic reached the booth where Jennifer and Linc stood, he stopped, standing with his feet firmly planted apart. His fists jammed on his hips, he glared at Jennifer, ignoring Linc. "Didn't you get the message?" he said again.

"Y . . . yes," Jennifer said, hating her own meekness.

"Then why didn't you return to the Rainbow?"

"Because . . . because . . ." She broke off. Why indeed hadn't she returned? Linc hadn't forced her to stay here. "We . . . we were going to eat . . . while the food was hot. . . ." Again she stopped. Dominic had turned his icy stare to their table where nothing remained except the two partially empty wine glasses. While they had been dancing, the waitress must have taken away their plates.

"It appears more likely you were drinking than eating," Dominic accused.

This was too much. Now he was doubting her word. It was all that was needed to turn her anxiety into anger to match his own.

Lifting her chin to meet his eyes with defiance, she said, "Today is my day off. My time is my own."

His heavy brows drew closer together over the high bridge of his nose. "Tomorrow is not your day off though."

"I'll be back in plenty of time to go to work tomorrow."

"Will you? You don't know these mountain storms. I'm thinking of your safety."

Jennifer cocked her head to one side, challenging him with her look. "Don't you think I'm capable of taking care of myself?"

"Frankly, no. Already that chair's dangerous to ride." Dominic swung his head around to glare at Linc. Then with a jerk of his hand he motioned toward the door. "Go on back up, Linc. I'll take care of your girl friend."

"I'm not . . ." Jennifer began, but broke off to watch Linc's departure. In spite of Linc's talk of defiance, he meekly obeyed Dominic's order and, without a word or a backward glance, he left the restaurant. Jennifer was now on her own with the angry Dominic Martin.

"I'll have to pay the bill." She snapped the words at him.

"Forget it. They'll put it on my charge."

"At least, allow me to gather up my possessions. Then I'll be ready to return to the Rainbow." Without waiting for his reply, she jerked away from him and reached into the booth to redeem her hat and her windbreaker. Jamming her hat onto her head, she refused his offer to help her into her jacket, and not bothering to zip it up, she raised her chin high and marched from the restaurant.

Outside, the wind caught Jennifer and took away her breath. Dominic came from behind and grasped her arm to help guide her. As she grabbed the brim of her hat with both hands to keep it from being swept away, she jerked Dominic's hand up along with the arm he held so firmly.

"Take that silly thing off your head and put up the hood of your jacket!" he said.

Jennifer resented the way he downgraded her hat as much as she resented his ordering her about. But now was no time to argue, and trying to keep the hat on her head was admittedly impractical. All her energy and concentration were needed to keep up with his lengthy stride. She snatched the hat from her head. To her surprise, Dominic helped her pull up the hood of her windbreaker.

Then he strode on ahead, pausing briefly to shout at her above the blustering wind, "You and Linc must have quite a thing going between you, since you're buying his meals already."

He waited for her to catch up. Again he seized her arm in his strong grip, so she could not escape from him. She turned her head to glare at him. "My private life and what I do with it is really no concern of yours." It gave her a small sense of satisfaction that Dominic Martin was irritated because she had offered to pay the bill for Linc's lunch. Brushing the snowflakes from her face, she added, "Linc did a favor for me. I wanted to show my appreciation."

"You needn't try to explain."

As if she needed to explain! Linc was only a friend. She had never yet met a man she could fall in love with. Not even the great Dominic Martin! She said, "I wasn't explaining!"

"Well, better save your breath for walking. We've got to get back to the Rainbow before this storm breaks. And don't kid yourself. It's going to break very soon. That chair lift will be dangerous when it does."

Now it seemed to Jennifer that Dominic might have been right about the storm, and Linc wrong. But she didn't want Dominic to be right! She hated him, didn't she?

Oh, I hate all men! Jennifer thought. Already she was shivering in the biting wind and wishing she had worn her down-filled parka instead of the light windbreaker.

An icy wind blew the snow straight toward their faces, the flakes stinging as they hit her cheeks.

An uncontrollable shiver shook her. Dominic turned his head to frown down at her. "Is that all you wore?"

She nodded. "It was warm and sunny this morning."

He swore under his breath. "Then for God's sake zip it all the way up. Why didn't you do that?"

"Because you're holding my arm in a death grip." The renewed anger sent warmth through her veins.

The wind whipped the hood of her windbreaker back off her head, and Jennifer stopped walking to try to pull it up again without releasing her hold on her pink hat.

Dominic frowned as he saw the difficulty she was having. "Here, let me take this thing." He reached out and took the hat to free her hands.

Jennifer released it reluctantly, and surprisingly, she saw Dominic laugh down into her face. "You're like a child with an ice cream cone. I'll only keep it for you, little girl. I promise I'll give it back."

He was grinning down at her, all traces of his anger gone. Without releasing his eyes from hers, he tucked the pink hat under his arm. Then he reached out to help her with the ties of her hood.

When the strings were securely fastened, Dominic caught both her shoulders. Jennifer felt the latent strength in his fingers. She knew she could not have escaped him if she had wanted to.

But somehow, she wasn't even sure that she wanted to. She knew now that he was right about the storm. That, she told herself, was the only reason she had been so willing to return with Dominic Martin to the Rainbow.

But she could not deny the warmth that flooded her body as he bent his head to kiss her full lips.

"What little boy, holding his girl's ice cream cone, could resist taking a lick?" he murmured, his smiling lips against her cold cheek. He adjusted her hood more securely. "Now come, we have to hurry to catch that chair lift."

Jennifer was too stunned to sort out her feelings. Especially as Dominic had immediately taken her arm and was propelling her even faster through the snow. Now, his mind was completely concentrated on reaching the chair lift. Though the snowflakes were whirring around Jennifer's face, her lips were slightly parted, still warmed by the memory of that unexpected kiss.

Chapter Five

They had almost reached the lower platform of the chair lift. The last hundred yards took them sharply uphill and, after the fast walk through the village, Jennifer was breathless. The path was icy and her feet slipped on it.

Dominic turned and easily picked her up, carrying her the remainder of the way to the loading platform.

The chairs appeared to be deserted, as far as Jennifer could tell through the increasing snowfall. The young attendant was jumping lightly from one foot to the other, blowing on the fingers of his bare hands.

"Thank God you're here at last, Mr. Martin," he said when he saw them. "I was afraid you wouldn't make it before we had to close down."

With only one glance at the boy, Dominic jerked his

own gloves from his pocket and tossed them to him. "You need them worse than I do."

The boy caught them, protesting, "Hey, man, you can't give away your gloves. You'll need . . ."

"Forget it. I'll be upstairs before my hands can get cold."

Jennifer saw the boy's gratitude as he thanked Dominic. Truly, Dominic Martin was the most unpredictable person she had ever encountered.

As they waited in position for the next oncoming chair, Dominic said, "Don't take any more passengers, Andy. As soon as you get the buzzer saying we're up, turn off the power and go home. No more chairs until this storm is over."

The chair came then, picked them up, and swept them up into the storm.

From behind came Andy's voice, "Good luck! Hope you make it."

"We will, Andy, we will." Dominic Martin's voice rang out into the falling snow.

From the seat beside her he turned to grin down at Jennifer. "You show considerable improvement in getting onto the lift since the last time I took you up."

She was glad the wind and cold had already brought blood to her cheeks, for the embarrassing memory of that other ride would undoubtedly have reddened them anyway. She said, "I've learned a lot of things in a week." She even wondered if there might be things she had not realized she was learning.

Jennifer wasn't certain whether the wind increased as their chair was carried up the mountain, or if the greater exposure to the elements at the higher altitude made the chair sway more and more. Her gloved hands grasped the rod across their laps, her fingers clutching it to brace herself against the onslaught of the wind's force. The rigidity of her grip seemed to help control her terrified shivering that jerked her body as the icy blasts struck her.

Dominic inched himself closer to her on the chair and put his arm around her, drawing her close to the warmth of his body.

Gratefully, Jennifer huddled close to him. With his outside hand, Dominic fished into the pocket of his jacket and pulled out a long woolen scarf, which he wrapped around her ears and the lower part of her face.

Above the length of dark wool Jennifer thanked him with her eyes, squinting against the sting of blowing snowflakes and cutting wind. The scarf held her windbreaker's hood closed now whereas before the wind had whipped in.

Dominic leaned close to shout above the increasing whine of the wind, "There's an old belief among outdoorsmen, 'If your feet are cold, put on your hat.' It's true too."

It was true. With her head and ears warmed by the scarf, Jennifer felt warmer. She noted that Dominic had followed his own advice, for the hood of his jacket had been raised to cover the fire of his hair. It was the first time Jennifer had seen him cover his head.

But as their chair rose still farther and the snowstorm increased, not even the protection of his scarf was enough. Jennifer pressed closer to Dominic, fitting her body into the curve of his arm.

As uncomfortable as the weather made her, she felt a

surge of warmth generated by this close contact. She was glad Dominic Martin was beside her, and not Linc.

It was his physical strength and his competence that impressed her, she told herself firmly. The storm made riding the chair lift dangerous. Hadn't Dominic said as much to the attendant on the platform below? She needed someone strong to give her confidence in this situation. It was that and nothing more that brought courage and warmth to her now.

When the chair ground to an abrupt halt, leaving them dangling helplessly suspended from a now motionless cable and no more than halfway up the mountainside to Rainbow Ridge, Jennifer's newly gained confidence drained away. Had the electricity gone off?

She turned her head to stare, wide-eyed, over the woolen scarf at Dominic. Through the scarf's fibers she said, "What happened?"

He was swearing softly. He broke off to look at her, obviously surprised. He had forgotten, until she spoke, that she was beside him. "The damned power's gone off. The storm, of course. And here I am stranded. . . . Ought to be upstairs . . ."

The blue ice of his stare cut through her as if he had said, *It's all because of you!*

It was true, of course. If it hadn't been for her, he would not have come down to the village.

But something within her seemed to snap. Shouldering the entire blame was just too much. Defying the bitter cold, she pushed herself away from him to glare at him. "Look, I didn't ask you to come down and get me!"

"Then why didn't you obey the orders I sent down to the village?"

No job, no matter how much she liked it, was worth being humiliated this way. She said through stiff lips, "Because I'm not used to being ordered around. I don't have to put up with that. Not even from you!" But the cold wind was sapping her physical strength, and a knot of fear had begun to form inside her. If the power remained off, they could freeze out here in the open, too far above the snow to even consider jumping. In desperate need of Dominic Martin's support, Jennifer began to make excuses. "Besides, Linc said . . ."

"Linc!" Dominic's angry shout told her, too late, that this was the wrong approach. "That's the very reason . . ." He broke off as violent shudders, one after another, shook Jennifer.

The effect on him was instantaneous. His anger evaporated and he reached out to draw her close again. "Oh, you poor kid. You're scared to death, aren't you?"

"No. I'm j-j-just . . . c-c-cold." She lowered her eyelids and tried to force back the threatening tears.

Dominic's motions were skillfully smooth and slow. Careful not to upset their balance on the open chair, he reached out and gently eased Jennifer close. Somehow he was able, in spite of the restraining bar, to get her legs across his so that she was sitting on his lap and he could enfold her in his arms.

She snuggled into his arms and buried her head in the curve of his shoulder.

"You're so cold." Dominic's voice sounded soft in her ear. He slid his free hand under her jacket to rub her back. His hand was warm even though he had given his gloves to the lift attendant. Her flesh tingled beneath the touch of his fingers. With his other hand he gently slipped the scarf away from her face. Once more his lips claimed hers and she surrendered to his deep kiss.

Now hot blood raced through her veins. The storm as well as the danger of their precarious position faded from her consciousness. She could feel, through the multiple layers of cloth and down, the warmth of his thighs against her own. For a moment, she abandoned herself to Dominic's embrace. She was suspended in time, high up above the earth.

Abruptly, the bubble burst as Dominic eased her back into a more decorous position. More shaken by passion than she had been by the cold, Jennifer felt the sharp hurt of rejection.

"The power's on again!" he shouted in triumph. Sure enough, the chairs were moving again, carrying them up the mountain.

New and unaccustomed feelings now raged in Jennifer. Without thinking, she lashed out at Dominic, "You can turn off and on. . . ." She broke off. She had been ready to accuse him of turning his own emotions on and off as easily as one turns a switch. But abruptly she realized that this would be an admission that her own emotions were not so easily controlled. This she knew she must not do.

Dominic misinterpreted her half-completed statement. "I didn't turn the power off, and from here I couldn't turn it on. It's the storm. You'll find our power is as fickle as a woman's love." He grinned at her. "Now why don't you move over and get ready for our landing? I doubt that you'll freeze now."

"Of course I won't freeze!" Jennifer was indignant. The nerve of the man to make love to her with such enjoyment and then pretend that nothing had happened! Well, she would show him! As far as she was concerned, nothing *had* happened. And nothing would again. She would see to that!

"Lift your feet, Jennifer!" Dominic's command broke into her thoughts. She obeyed instantly. Now she knew of the danger of dangling feet when the edge of the upper platform approached.

Within seconds they stood safely on the solid platform boards. "Stop the chair," Dominic called out. "We'll take no more chances tonight."

Jennifer heard the chair's engine grind to a slow halt as at last the chairs hung motionless from the cable.

"Thank heavens you made it before the power goes off for good," a voice said out of the thick curtain of falling snowflakes. Jennifer could barely make out the dim shape of the attendant bundled against the cold and snow-filled wind.

"Of course we made it!" Dominic's voice was coolly offhand. "You didn't think I'd remain stranded out there all night, did you?"

Again the arrogant male! thought Jennifer. He was really impossible!

And yet part of her felt he was correct. Not even the elements would dare to defy Dominic Martin!

Groping through the heavy snowfall she hurried toward the warmth of the lodge. Inwardly she vowed to herself that she would never again allow Dominic to hold complete power over her.

Before she could grasp the door's handle, his familiar voice came to her from behind. "Next time you go downstairs, for Pete's sake, Jennifer, wear enough clothing!"

Without bothering to answer him, Jennifer moved away, only to find her pink hat thrust unceremoniously into her hand.

"Here's something you forgot," he said.

She snatched the hat from his hand. "Thanks." She flung open the door and stepped into the lodge. Dominic followed close behind her.

Jennifer had scarcely entered the lodge when Cassie came up. Her glance flicked over Jennifer, lingering for a second on the pink hat, then looked beyond her at Dominic who was stamping his snowy boots by the door.

"Oh, Dominic! I've been s-o-o-o worried about you. Thank God you're safe!" She ran past Jennifer and flung herself into Dominic Martin's arms.

Jennifer could not resist turning her head to watch. She saw Dominic open his arms and enfold Cassie in them just as so brief a time ago he had enfolded her.

The sudden pain that stabbed through Jennifer was physical. She started to hurry away to her own room. She did not want anyone to see how she felt. Cassie's strident voice brought her to a halt.

"Don't go away yet, Jennifer dear," Cassie trilled. "I'm simply dying to hear the exciting story of how Linc rescued that adorable pink hat for you."

Like a sharply focused picture on a television screen, the signs dotting the face of the mountain sprang into Jennifer's mind. *"Skiing forbidden"* they read.

How much did Cassie know about Linc's illicit venture down the snowy mountain face? And what did she plan to do with this knowledge?

"Oh, Dominic," Cassie murmured again as she nuzzled against his shoulder. "You'll never know how worried I was. Already it's almost dark, and just thinking of you out there in the freezing darkness, all alone. . . . Oh, I can't bear it!"

"I wasn't all alone, Cassie," Dominic said dryly, "Jennifer was with me."

Although Jennifer could not see Cassie's face, she could see the stiffening of her shoulders. A soft laugh bubbled up from deep in her throat, as she said, "Oh, yes. You did go down to make Jennifer come back, didn't you? My, didn't she make all you men jump through a hoop!"

Dominic disengaged Cassie's arms from his neck, then held her off to look into her eyes. "Just what do you mean by that, Cassie?"

"Well, I mean, Linc couldn't wait to ski down the face to rescue her hat! He knows how Jennifer adores that hat. He ought to know. He gave it to her in the first place. And when . . . Oh." With her hand covering her mouth and her eyes wide, Cassie turned to say to Jennifer, "Am I telling a secret? Something I shouldn't?"

Jennifer was too angry to trust herself to reply, but as Cassie had expected, Dominic rose to her bait. He stepped around her and strode over to Jennifer, jabbing his finger accusingly at the pink hat clutched in her hands. "This hat?"

Jennifer opened her mouth but no words came out. No matter what she said, she would be found guilty. If she denied owning the pink hat, everyone, Dominic included, would know she lied. If she admitted it was hers she would have to admit that Linc had rescued it, breaking one of Dominic's most rigid rules by skiing the forbidden face. There was no denying the fact that Linc had rescued her hat, and he would be blamed for it. And she would be blamed too, for failing in her duty to see that the ski instructors followed the rules. And Dominic himself had reminded her that this was one of her duties.

Cassie had done a thorough job of getting her in trouble, bad trouble.

But now Dominic towered over her, waiting for her to answer his question. His fists were jammed on his hips and his eyebrows had drawn so close together they almost met on his forehead.

Cassie said, "I didn't mean to get anyone in trouble. Truly I didn't, Dominic." The long lashes fluttered as she looked up at him.

I'll just bet you didn't! Jennifer thought.

Dominic said, "I'll be the judge of who's in trouble. Answer my question, Jennifer. Is this the hat all the fuss is about?"

"Yes." The word seemed to be swallowed up by the ominous silence that followed.

Jennifer was astonished to see how many people in the lounge had turned to watch the scene in which she was a principal actor. She glanced anxiously from one face to another. They seemed to stare their accusation at her. The silence stretched out endlessly.

At last Dominic continued his questioning. "And did the hat blow off your head as you rode the big chair down to the village?"

"Yes." All that was necessary, she thought, was a witness stand to make this into a courtroom. Humiliation had turned to defensive anger when Dominic said,

"Then come to my office. I'll hear your side of the story first."

He turned on his heel and headed toward the open door.

For an instant Jennifer stood where she was, tempted to defy him. Yet she knew she had to obey, if only to persuade him to deal compassionately with Linc's misdemeanor.

Dominic stopped and looked back over his shoulder. "Well? Are you coming, or aren't you?"

The sharpness in his eyes told her there would be little compassion for her, yet she felt obliged to follow him. She carefully avoided meeting Cassie's glance as she walked, head high, across the room. She did not need to look at Cassie's face to guess the gleeful triumph reflected there.

Dominic held the door open while Jennifer walked past him into his office. Once inside, she stood in the center of the floor, her rigidly straight back confronting him as he entered and closed the door.

He strode ahead of her and seated himself at his desk.

"Well?" he inquired coldly.

Jennifer looked down at the thick carpet. She did not want to face Dominic's open hostility yet. But she couldn't let Cassie get away with her accusation that she had asked Linc to rescue her hat.

Still without looking up, she said, "How could I have sent word for Linc to ski down for my hat? I was on the chair going down to the village. No way to communicate with anyone. And he got to the village so soon he must have started down while I was still on the chair."

"Did I accuse you of sending Linc for your hat?"

Now Jennifer flashed him a look of accusation. "No, but Cassie did, and you believed her."

"Are you sure Cassie said that?" His voice was deceptively soft.

"No, but she implied it."

Dominic sprang to his feet, slamming both his palms on the desk with such force it startled her. "Good God, Jennifer, will you stop beating that theme to death!"

She clenched her hands into fists but managed to hold them rigidly against her thighs.

With a slashing motion of his hand, as if to dismiss that subject, he went on, "Oh, why in heaven's name am I arguing with you about that! Your part in Linc's rescue of the hat isn't the main issue anyway."

Dominic Martin strode around from behind his desk and came to face her. Both his hands were jammed into the pockets of his trousers as he glared down at her. "You ran off to the village half naked in weather . . ."

"I wasn't half naked! I had on clothes! And the weather was lovely! I had on my . . ."

"I don't give a hoot what you wore, it wasn't enough! And you've been here long enough by now to know better than to wear a stupid confection like that hat when you're riding the big chair!" He was shouting so loudly that her attempts to interrupt were lost. "You might expect it to blow off. Anyway, it wouldn't have given you any more warmth than a piece of mosquito netting. It's good for nothing! You could have caught pneumonia! Don't you ever learn?"

Jennifer had had all she could take. The tension that had been building up in her broke, and a torrent of words burst from her like water from a dam.

"Of course I learn! The first time I walked into this

lodge I learned in an instant that a silly hat might make me look a little more like the others here. I'd made a mistake on my clothes and I couldn't afford to correct that, but I could afford what you call a stupid confection of a hat. I needed something to restore the confidence that you and . . . and . . . others had robbed me of." Jennifer heard her own voice rising in pitch, but she could not stop herself.

"Linc understood my problem," she went on. "He's human, and you're nothing but a machine, Dominic Martin! I'll starve before I'll let a computer like you run my life. I'm quitting my job. I'm leaving this place right now!" She swung away from him before the tears she had only just managed to hold back should burst from her.

"Oh, you're leaving, are you, Jennifer?" he said, and she heard the edge of sarcasm in his voice. "Just how do you expect to leave the Rainbow? The big chair has been stopped by my orders, and it won't be started up again until I give further orders." He broke off, fixing her with a hard glare.

Jennifer stifled an involuntary gasp by catching her lower lip between her teeth. Of course, he was right. What a fool she had been to expect to get the better of Dominic Martin!

Dominic was speaking again. "No matter how much I might want you out of my hair, I wouldn't send my worst enemy down on that chair tonight. It's too dangerous in this storm." His eyes were glacier hard as they held hers, and he added, "Perhaps your friend Linc will have another idea?"

Jennifer could feel the blood pounding at her temples. "I'll find a way to get down. Don't worry. I wouldn't spend another night under the same roof with you. . . ."

"Just see that Linc doesn't get you to spend it with him," he said.

The man was brutal! Jennifer's hands clenched into fists, and she was so angry she might have struck out at him except that suddenly the room was plunged into complete darkness. The power he had called fickle was proving his words. It had gone off again.

The effect on Dominic Martin was instant and unexpected. Through the thick darkness Jennifer heard his quick intake of breath and then his laughter rippled across to her. "So, you'll find a way to get down, will you, my fiery Jennifer? In the darkness and with no electric power? I doubt now that we'll have power for the remainder of the night, perhaps even longer. Short of sprouting your own wings, there's no way you can leave the Rainbow tonight. I doubt if your friend Linc can fly away either!"

"Oh!" she cried. "I hate you!" Jennifer swung around and groped for the door.

She had not expected to find darkness so complete, so intense. The room was not familiar enough to her to orient herself, and Jennifer was afraid she might blunder again into the wrong doorway. She did not want to stumble into Dominic's bedroom again. She had been humiliated enough.

As she hesitated, trying to remember on which side of her lay the way to her room, she felt his hands grasp her shoulders. She had not heard him approach, and his touch made her stiffen.

He turned her around gently.

She assumed he was turning her to face the doorway

into the corridor. But then she felt his warm breath on her cheek, and she knew he had swung her around to face him. The effect of his nearness was devastating, sending her into an unbidden confusion.

Out of the darkness came Dominic's voice. "So, I'm a machine, am I, Jennifer? A coldhearted computer?"

His arms slid around her, pressing her close to him as his mouth came down to claim hers. His tongue brushed her lips, forcing them apart in spite of her efforts to remain distant. His muscular thighs strained warm against her.

At first Jennifer tried to struggle against him, but his strength was far greater than hers, and there was a part of her that did not wish to struggle. The heat of his thighs pressing against her own made passion rise in her to respond to his. She relaxed in his arms and her kisses became as fiery as his.

"Oh, Jennifer," he murmured against her ear. "Why do we waste time in anger?"

Though she could not have spoken a word even had she wanted to, they were interrupted by loud knocking on the door, and Cassie's voice called out, "Dominic, did the lights go out in there too?"

Dominic released his hold on Jennifer, but before he opened the door he inquired mockingly, "Do you still consider me a machine?" Once more she was speechless.

Cassie's voice, demanding now, came to them. "Dominic! Can you hear me? What are you doing . . . ?"

The door swung open, and the faint and flickering light that came from the corridor outside spotlighted Jennifer.

"Oh, Dominic," Cassie cried. "I was afraid you were . . ." She giggled.

Dominic, unperturbed, said, "I'm ready to talk to Linc now. The power failure won't interfere with that. Will you go get him for me, Cassie?"

Jennifer caught the venom of Cassie's glance as she turned away to do Dominic's bidding.

Dominic pressed a flashlight into her hands. She knew that he had guessed she would want to scurry off to her room without facing Cassie again.

In an effort to show that she too was unruffled, she said, "Don't be too hard on Linc."

Not even the dimness of the lighting hid the warning lights that came on in Dominic's eyes. "Jennifer, this computer has a large memory bank stored full of information on the care and feeding of Linc's temperament. Don't blow its circuit by trying to intercede."

A returning rush of anger made Jennifer swing away to stride off down the corridor. No, she thought, Dominic's fiery kisses had not disproved her accusation that he was a machine. He had kissed her only to demonstrate to her the power he had over her emotions. Surely, nowhere in the world could she find a man who could so drive her to distraction! She could hardly wait to reach the privacy of her room to get him out of her sight. He was all Cassie's—if she wanted him. *They deserve each other,* she thought spitefully.

Chapter Six

The next morning there was still no electric power. As soon as Jennifer had dressed in warm slacks of wool in a bright red-and-black plaid with a black pullover brightened by a red scarf, she hurried to the kitchen to see if Cook needed help in preparing breakfast without electricity.

To her surprise she found not Cook but Dominic. He was bent over a low cabinet in a far corner of the kitchen, and he was pulling out antiquated cooking utensils.

Jennifer glanced around the large and well-equipped kitchen, and said, "Where's Cook?"

Dominic sat back on his heels. He looked at her over his shoulder. "Cook's lost without his electronic modern miracles," he explained. "When the electricity dies, Cook dies."

"You don't have gas as a standby?" she asked.

"Of course not. Too much fire hazard, especially in summer during dry spells."

"Then what are you going to do?"

"I'll manage," he said.

He would too, she knew. That was part of the maddening thing about Dominic Martin. But now Jennifer was interested in just how he would manage.

Among the pieces of old-fashioned equipment Dominic brought out was a large kettle. As soon as Jennifer saw it she knew it had been designed for use over an open fire.

She was intrigued. "What will we cook in it?"

"*I'll* cook my famous stew. *You* can cope with breakfast." She did not fail to catch his emphasis on the personal pronouns.

Of course *he* would cook the main meal. Dominic Martin needed no one, cared about no one, except, of course, Cassie.

Without another word Jennifer gathered up bowls and boxes of cereal and left the kitchen. So the All Powerful wished to cook in the kitchen, did he? Heaven forbid that she would get in his way! Nevertheless, not even the rich cream that was available for the dry cereal, nor the fresh fruit and steaming coffee poured from the huge enameled coffeepot Dominic himself wielded at the fireplace gave her the satisfaction she craved.

Word got around quickly that Cook had retired to his room for the duration of the power problem, defeated and disheartened by being deprived of his electronic equipment. The guests cooperated by scraping their plates and burning in the fireplace whatever was combustible.

Jennifer gathered up the leftovers and carried them back to the kitchen.

Dominic was there, busily cutting up vegetables for his stew. Without turning around he said, "You didn't think I could cook, did you?"

"Is there anything you can't do?" she parried sarcastically.

"There are things I haven't tried." His voice was casual.

"I'm amazed," she said, not masking the cynical tone in her voice.

He swung around to fix her with his gaze. "Envious?"

His motion was so unexpected she didn't have time to compose her facial muscles. "Of course not!"

He did not pursue that point, but said instead, "Maybe someday I'll try one of those things I haven't tried yet."

Jennifer found the intensity of his gaze too disconcerting. Without another word she turned and left the room.

During the morning the guests entertained themselves. As lunchtime drew near, Jennifer sensed their growing restlessness. They had paid good money to come here and enjoy the snowy outdoors, but the storm continued and Dominic Martin would allow no one to go out into it.

Even Jennifer felt this was undue restraint, and her own impatience made it more difficult for her to keep morale at a good professional level.

But as she moved quickly between groups, suggesting table tennis tournaments, offering a game board to a couple who appeared at loose ends, she was shocked by a loud crash. It reverberated through the lodge. The building shook.

Instant silence followed, holding the lounge's occupants for seconds as in a spell. Jennifer spun around toward the source from which the sound seemed to come.

Her eyes met the enigmatic stare of Dominic Martin. Had he been watching her as she worked? She felt her heartbeat quicken. *Blast him!* she thought for the hundredth time.

"That crash was only snow falling from the roof," he said calmly. "That's why I insist that everyone stay inside during the storm until we can clear the roof off. If someone had happened to be standing there . . ." A shrug of his shoulders eloquently completed his thought.

The group's comprehension of the danger was expressed in the nervous chatter and joking that broke out. Some of the jokes were macabre, Jennifer thought, graphically predicting what might have happened if specific persons had stood under the eaves when all those tons of snow came down.

But the incident enabled the guests to be more philosophical about their confinement. The remainder of the morning passed without incident.

Noontime brought another of Dominic Martin's timely ideas to light. From the cabinet in the kitchen he produced old-fashioned corn poppers with long handles designed for use over an open fire. The guests clamored for turns at popping the corn. With it, bright, crisp apples were served along with steaming coffee, hot chocolate and fresh milk. He passed around platters of cookies that had been made before the power failure. The meal was a success, and Dominic was again the hero of the moment. Jennifer could not help admiring the calm way he handled the emergency situations.

His calmness had an effect on her too. She redoubled her efforts to keep the guests amused. She introduced a game of charades that met with such enthusiastic response it soon turned into an amateur theatrical performance.

When the evening meal was served, Jennifer enjoyed Dominic's stew as much as the guests did. The hot meal refreshed her, and she went back to work after dinner with renewed vigor.

By the time the guests began to go to their rooms, however, Jennifer was exhausted. She had not seen Dominic since earlier in the afternoon. Others from his staff had served the stew he had prepared.

Word went around that Dominic Martin was working outdoors with two of his maintenance crew removing the snow from the roof. Jennifer had scarcely found time to wonder or worry about him. She told herself she should feel relief that he wasn't standing around looking over her shoulder and criticizing her work.

At last she was free to go to her room for some much needed sleep and rest. The hour was late and she had been up since very early morning. The exhaustion was beginning to tell on her.

As she approached her door she saw that a strip of light shone under it. There seemed to be a light on in the room. Jennifer frowned. Had the electricity been restored? She had been especially careful to extinguish her lamp. Not only did leaving it on use up the limited supply of fuel, but there was always the danger of fire when any kind of flame was left untended. Jennifer hurried as she covered the last distance to the door of her room.

As she pushed the door open, she stifled a gasp. In one of the two big upholstered chairs Dominic Martin sprawled, his long legs stretched out across the matching ottoman. His head lay back against the chair's cushion and his closed eyelids hid the blue of his eyes while his massive chest rose and fell rhythmically in sleep.

A smile Jennifer couldn't suppress played around her mouth as she tiptoed across to look down at him. Sleep had softened the planes of his face erasing most of the weariness. He appeared younger, surprisingly vulnerable.

Something within Jennifer seemed to turn over, and her throat closed as if to shut off her breathing. What was happening to her, she wondered. What had Dominic Martin done to her?

She gave her shoulders a shake forcing herself to be practical. Quietly, she went to her bed and stripped two wool blankets from it. She brought one back and laid it over Dominic Martin, gently tucking it around him, careful not to disturb his sleep. He did not stir. She knew he must be very tired.

When the blanket had been adjusted to her satisfaction, she carried the other blanket back to the second upholstered chair and curled up in that with the blanket around her.

Before she dropped off to sleep, Jennifer wondered what had brought Dominic here to her room. It occurred to her that he might have come to reprimand her for allowing the guests to borrow from the lodge's supplies to improvise costumes for their theatricals.

Not another fight with him! The thought was more than she could bear.

But even this worry was not enough to keep her awake. The long day had exhausted her. She was soon fast asleep.

Jennifer was startled into wakefulness by being lifted from her position. She had no idea what time it was, or where she was. Then she remembered going to sleep in the chair. When Dominic Martin claimed her lips with his own, she sprang into full wakefulness. She felt herself being carried from the chair and laid on her bed.

The sleep, brief though it may have been, left her relaxed, her defenses lowered. She responded to his kiss, allowing her arms to steal up and encircle him; her soft lips yielded to his demanding firmness.

With a groan he flung his length onto the bed beside her and drew her close. She adjusted to the curve of his body, abandoning all caution as she clung to him.

Abruptly, Dominic broke her hold on him and sprang to his feet to stand glaring down at her. Lying on the bed, her emotions in turmoil, Jennifer saw the sparks of anger flicker in his eyes. His chest rose and fell with his labored breathing.

"Was this a trick, Jennifer?" he demanded.

"What . . . what do you mean?"

"Did you trick me into taking advantage of you? Were you awake all the time I was carrying you to this bed?"

The sudden emptiness of her arms when he pulled away had left a hollow inside her: his accusation now filled it with an agony of hurt.

She swung her legs over the side of the bed to bring herself into a sitting position. "Of course it wasn't a trick!" She paused in an attempt to stop the trembling she heard in her own voice. "I was asleep. I was in the middle of a dream, a lovely dream, and you . . . and you . . . You had no right to come to my room . . . without . . . I didn't invite you into my room!" With the greatest effort she managed to stop herself from saying, *I didn't invite you into my dream either.*

She must not let him see how he had stirred her emotions. She was thankful that whatever the reason, he had stopped their lovemaking before it was too late. But oh, the humiliation of knowing it was he, not she, who broke them apart!

Dominic ran his hand through his shock of red hair. He smiled ruefully; his shoulders sagged as if fatigue had again caught up with him. "I guess we were both too exhausted to know what we were doing. I suggest we forget all about it, okay?"

Jennifer nodded her head. She could not bring herself to make a verbal agreement, for she knew that she could never forget the lovely feeling of waking to find Dominic Martin making love to her.

Her nod seemed to satisfy him. He crossed the room to the door. Jennifer followed him, reaching him just as the door swung open under his hand.

Then, as if he had only just remembered, he turned back to her, whispering into the quiet of the sleeping lodge, "I came here to thank you for pitching in the way you did today. Good job, Jennifer."

He bent down, and with his index finger lifted her chin. The kiss he placed on her lips was gentle but firm. Then he was gone, his long legs striding down the dimly lighted corridor.

For a time Jennifer remained in the doorway, her emotions in turmoil.

Forget all about it, he had said.

Of course Dominic Martin meant nothing by his lovemaking. The passions of such a dynamic, virile man would naturally be stirred easily, and just as easily turned in another direction. It would be ridiculous and naive for Jennifer to read any meaning into his visit to her room and his subsequent actions.

She gave a quick start as she became aware of a shadow moving in the faint light that spread out into the corridor from her room. Or was it a shadow? It was gone almost as quickly as Jennifer became aware of it, but she had been certain it was a person, someone who slipped quickly from one darkened doorway to another.

Had someone been watching Dominic and Jennifer as they kissed in the lighted doorway?

As always, Jennifer's suspicions fastened on Cassie. It was always Cassie who waited, like an animal stalking its prey, to find a way to blacken Jennifer's name. Had Cassie seen Dominic with her in her room tonight?

A sickness that was almost physical swept over Jennifer at the thought. Who knew what mischief

Cassie would make of the innocent scene she had witnessed?

But had it been completely innocent? At the memory of her own response to Dominic's lovemaking, a rush of warm blood flooded up the column of Jennifer's throat and into her face.

Chapter Seven

By the following morning the storm had for the most part abated. The wind had died down, and lazy snowflakes floated gently to the ground, to become lost in the snowpack that was already many feet deep.

Being confined, now that the storm had largely ended, was harder on the guests than when the wind had raged. Dominic had given strict orders that no one could leave the lodge except to chunk snow.

He had taken his maintenance crew up onto the roof. Here they sectioned off the snow into chunks, broke the chunks off from the mass, and sent them sliding down the incline of the steeply pitched roof to fall harmlessly onto the ground.

Dominic spent the morning outside, occasionally coming inside to gulp down a mug of scalding coffee.

His work gloves were soaked through and his hands red with cold. His face was beaded with sweat from the heavy exercise, yet he appeared tireless in his efforts.

The ski instructors took their turns too at this chunking. The coffeepot was filled and emptied time and time again.

Jennifer was refilling it to set it back on the fire to heat again when one of the ski instructors said in an aside to her, "What's this I hear about you and The Man, Jennifer?"

She met his gaze squarely. "I've no idea. What did you hear?"

His grin was full of mischief. "None of the other women have got him to spend the night with them, though many have tried. Wow, what a way you must have!"

Laughing, he started away, but Jennifer grabbed his arm, sloshing water from the coffeepot to hiss into the fire. "Now just wait a minute. It wasn't like that at all, and if that kind of rumor's going around, I want you to kill it right now. Was it Cassie who told you?" she demanded.

"I don't rat on anybody," he said, but she guessed from the evasive look on his face that she was correct. With another admonition to stop the rumor, she let him go, but she was raging inside.

A little later she met Cassie in the hall. Although she was tempted to confront Cassie with the accusation of starting a false rumor, Jennifer knew it would do no good and might cause her to lose her own temper. She gave Cassie an impersonal smile and started to go on.

Cassie stepped in front of her, blocking her way, and said, "I'm surprised you didn't sleep in this morning after your late night."

Jennifer raised her eyebrows. "My late night? I went to my room about the same time you and everyone else did. We all had a long day."

"It wasn't what time you went to your room," Cassie taunted. "It was how late Dominic stayed there with you. Do you invite all your boyfriends to spend the night with you? Has Linc also enjoyed the privilege?"

Jennifer managed to hold back her rage at Cassie as she countered, "Have you asked Dominic if I invited him there?"

"Of course not."

"Then I suggest you consult with him before you circulate rumors about me." Jennifer stepped around Cassie and walked away, carefully keeping her steps measured and smooth. She hoped Cassie had not seen her angry flush. Now she knew beyond any doubt that the shadowy figure she had seen in the hallway the night before had been Cassie.

But another, more disconcerting thought occurred to her. Perhaps the shadowy figure had indeed been nothing more than a shadow, but when Dominic left her room he had gone to Cassie and the two of them had joked about how easily Jennifer had succumbed to him.

Immediately Jennifer blamed herself for being unduly suspicious. *It's my nerves,* she told herself. She was as susceptible as the guests to the tension of being confined in the lodge. And she had the additional responsibilities of her job.

For the time being the guests all seemed to be occupied, and Jennifer fled to the tiny cubicle that had been assigned to her as an office. Here she could smooth the feathers that Cassie had so effectively ruffled. At the same time she could study the notes her predecessor had left. Perhaps from them she could glean one or two fresh ideas for keeping the guests happy.

Inside the office, she sank into the chair behind her desk. It was good to escape even briefly from the others, to steal a few moments of relaxation before she plunged into work again. She picked up the pages Lodi had left. For longer than she had intended, Jennifer studied the outlines. As she became involved in reading them, she detached herself from her surroundings.

With her head bent over the papers on her desk and her thoughts concentrated on a plan forming in her mind, she did not know that Dominic had come into her office until his thundering voice startled her.

"Just what are you doing in here?" he shouted. "There are people out there, girl, waiting for you!"

Jennifer stood up, white with anger. The nerve of the man! She had worked hard all morning. Why shouldn't she take a quick break? Had she taken the job to be insulted? First by the ski instructor, then by Cassie and now by Dominic himself.

She narrowed her eyes to meet his glowering look. "I am doing my job to the best of my ability, Mr. Martin," she retorted. "And if you are not satisfied, I am more than willing to leave, with suitable recompense, of course."

His blue eyes darkened until she felt as though she

must drown in their deep pools. He stepped forward. "Perhaps you would consider this suitable recompense, Miss Evans," he said mockingly, as his demanding lips claimed hers.

What had started out as a punishing kiss deepened as his probing tongue sought and found hers. The room spun around Jennifer. Like a twirling dancer she tried to focus on something fixed, but her world continued to whirl through space.

He released her abruptly, although his hands still gripped her shoulders, which was all that prevented her knees from collapsing beneath her.

"I'm not completely without heart, Jennifer," he said at last, his voice sounding more steady than her knees felt. "But the morning has been a long one and the idea that you were goofing off kind of got to me."

Anger rose again to give new strength to her legs, although as yet she was unable to speak.

He swung away from her as he said, "What I really came in here for was to tell you about the game closet downstairs." He explained that the games in this closet were kept for emergencies to be brought out, fresh and new, to the guests who had tired of every form of entertainment in the lodge's normal program. Handing Jennifer the key to the closet, he added, "It's the door you may have noticed between the first aid room and the ski shop, downstairs past the lockers."

This was a much-needed bonus, and Jennifer was too grateful to mention anything more at the moment about leaving the lodge. Moreover, her emotions were in such turmoil that she did not trust herself to continue that argument. Time enough for that later. She accepted the key with formal thanks, and when he had left, she tried to get back to work.

But her concentration had been destroyed. Had he kissed her to apologize for his loss of temper? Was it possible that he knew the effect his nearness had on her? The mere thought of this made Jennifer groan.

There was no use in trying to work in her office now. She couldn't even gather her thoughts together. With a sigh she rose to her feet, pocketing the key, having decided to save this treasure trove until a real moment of need. She went out to join the guests.

For a time she kept them interested in singing nostalgic songs. In the group she found a willing volunteer to play the piano, and after the first and boldest among the guests suggested songs from their past, interest grew.

Jennifer managed to keep the crowd amused with one idea and another until lunchtime. The power had come on again and Cook was working happily with his electronic equipment. His efforts produced a luncheon menu worthy of a gourmet restaurant, at least it seemed so to Jennifer, contrasting it to the past days of improvisations.

After lunch she decided to delve into the treasure closet of games for which Dominic had given her the key.

She hurried downstairs. As she made her way through the corridor that led to the locker room, she saw Cassie and one of the maintenance crew approaching from the opposite direction. Cassie's companion wore a paint spattered coverall, and Cassie was clinging to his arm with one hand, while the other held a lighted cigarette.

Cassie grinned at Jennifer as they approached. "Hi, Jennifer," she said. "I've been helping Ben paint the first aid room. Haven't I been helping, Ben?" She turned to him, fluttering her eyelashes, and Jennifer saw the smear of paint on her cheek.

"You sure have been helping, Cassie," Ben said. "Wow!"

The two went on, giggling together as Cassie snuggled against him.

Jennifer hurried on into the locker room.

The room was dark, its tall banks of lockers standing like sentinels towering over her in the half-light. Jennifer did not know where the switch was, so she carefully threaded her way among the lockers.

But from ahead there came light, a flickering, dancing light. A buzz of warning sounded in Jennifer's mind, and she began to run toward the source of this light.

She knew without going into the room that there was fire inside the first aid room. But she had to open the door. She screamed as loud as she could, "Help! Fire!"

Then she flung the door open and, with her left arm instinctively protecting her face, stepped cautiously into the room.

The fire was burning in a wad of paint-soaked rags lying on the concrete floor. So far, it had not spread, but in the draft from the opening door it flared up. Jennifer eased around it and grabbed the blanket that lay across the foot of the cot. Shaking it to unfold it, she tossed it over the pile of rags, smothering the flames. In doing so, she exposed her arm to a flash of fire leaping out from under a blanket fold.

Although the synthetic fabric of her jersey did not catch fire, it dissolved in the heat, searing the flesh of Jennifer's arm.

Ignoring the pain, she worked with the blanket to make certain the fire was thoroughly extinguished. Fortunately, the flames had not spread throughout the room. Jennifer dared not comtemplate what could have happened if the paint rags had been closer to the cot's bedding.

When the ordeal was over, she sank onto the floor, exhausted and nauseated by the acrid odor of scorched wool and paint. Now she became aware of the intense pain in her arm. She closed her eyes and rested her head on her good right arm, laid across her bent knees.

She was sunk into a semi-stupor when she dimly heard running footsteps. Lifting heavy eyelids, she recognized Dominic Martin bending over her.

"Let's have a look at that arm," he said impersonally, as a doctor might have.

"It's nothing," she murmured, wincing as he pulled the burned edges of her sleeve from the flesh.

He helped her remove the turtleneck top that had been so fresh and becoming that morning. Now it was torn and ragged and reeked of smoke.

She made no protest over his disrobing her; his hands were gentle and knowing.

Yanking the sheet from the cot, he handed it to her to cover her bra and bare shoulders. With tenderness that surprised her he treated her burned arm, bandaged it, then gave her a sleeping pill.

"Now," he said when the job was done, "I'll get you back to your room. Someone else can take over your duties for the rest of the day. You'll need to rest."

"Don't you want to know about the fire?" she managed to say.

His expression hardened. "Not now. Plenty of time to deal with that after you've recovered a bit."

Deal with what? she wanted to ask. But her strength was gone, and she was more than willing to wait. Later she could piece together the details.

Dominic bent down and scooped Jennifer up in his arms, tucking the sheet protectively around her. He carried her out of the first aid room, closing and locking the door after them.

Jennifer thought she saw him pocket the key, and this puzzled her. But she was in no state to solve puzzles.

He carried her up the stairs, keeping to the back corridors and using the back stairway. He took her to her room and he laid her gently on the bed.

He stood over her, looking down at her as he said, "You're to stay there until tomorrow morning, Jennifer."

"Gladly," she said. She had meant to accompany the word with a laugh, but a sudden exhaustion overwhelmed her and she closed her eyes.

She could tell, however, that he was still standing over her. Faintly, the lemonish scent of him came to her nostrils and she sighed. She felt his lips brush first across one of her eyelids and then the other. Was it a dream, or had he muttered thickly, "Oh, Jennifer, when I think what could have happened to you—"

The latch clicked and she knew that she was alone. . . .

Later that night she woke up to wonder. Did Dominic hold her responsible for the fire in the first aid room? He knew that she had a key. Perhaps he thought she had carelessly lent it to one of the guests or staff. Abruptly her thoughts switched, and she remembered meeting Cassie and her friend in the corridor downstairs. Cassie had admitted being in the first aid room. She had boasted about helping to paint it. And Cassie's hand had held a lighted cigarette!

Now Jennifer worried whether she should tell Dominic the next morning what she had seen. She disliked intensely telling on someone, but wasn't this instance an exception, since it involved the lodge building itself?

Before she could resolve this debate in her mind, she fell into a dreamless sleep.

By morning both her injured arm and her spirits had been immeasurably restored. Although she still had not decided what to do, she felt certain that in the quiet and businesslike atmosphere of her office she would surely be able to make up her mind.

She dressed carefully so that her injured arm would have as little pressure from clothing as possible and yet she would be warm. A loose fitting sweater in wide stripes of varying colors worn over a white blouse with long sleeves to be a buffer against the abrasiveness of the wool seemed best, and with it she wore pants of solid yellow, the predominant color in the sweater pattern.

When she came into the dining room for breakfast,

the first person she met was Cassie. The encounter threatened to undermine her state of well-being.

"Good morning, Cassie," Jennifer said, attempting casualness.

Without responding, Cassie thrust out her lower lip and with a disdainful twitch of her shoulders turned away.

The two women stood side by side at the long table from which all, guests and staff alike, were expected to serve themselves at breakfast. Jennifer could not allow such a deliberate snub to go unchallenged. She said, "What have I done to deserve that kind of nongreeting, Cassie?"

Cassie turned on her with eyes that blazed with dislike. "As if you didn't know! Miss Pure-and-Innocent herself, aren't you?"

Jennifer sighed heavily. "Oh, Cassie, stop talking in riddles and let's get this thing straightened out."

Cassie picked up her laden tray. "Well, if you're too dumb to figure that one out, then I feel sorry for you." She walked away, swinging her hips with small jerks that emphasized her pique.

Again Jennifer sighed. Cassie with her moods wasn't worth worrying about, especially with the extra work that had piled up since the fire.

The guests were allowed to go outside again that day. They exploded into the outdoors, delighted to escape the restrictions of their involuntary confinement. The snow had piled so deep around the lifts that they had to be dug out before they could be put into operation. Many of the guests plunged into helping out with this work; a holiday spirit of cooperation prevailed. Jennifer longed to join in this fun, but her arm was still too painful to allow strenuous use and she had plenty to do inside, making plans for the evening's entertainment schedule.

It was probable that for another day or so the big chair would not be in operation, so no one could return to the village yet.

Jennifer still had to make a decision about whether or not to tell Dominic about seeing Cassie with a cigarette as she returned from the first aid room. She wanted to think that Cassie's bad mood had been caused by a reprimand from Dominic, that he had found out about her smoking so near the paint. That would solve her problem without putting her into the unenviable position of telling on Cassie.

But that was a false hope. There was no way Dominic could have known about that. And Jennifer was certain that Cassie would not confess to being the possible cause of the fire.

When she went to her office, Jennifer found a note on her desk from Dominic saying he wanted to see her immediately.

She stood for a moment frowning. Then she crumpled the paper into a small ball. The crackle of the paper gave her a little satisfaction, as if by doing it she had crushed Dominic's demand on her inmost thoughts.

Nevertheless, she hurried on to his office.

His head was bent over his desk when she entered through the open door.

Without looking up, he said, "Good morning, Jennifer. I hope you are feeling as good as you look."

How could he know about her appearance, since his eyes were focused on the papers on his desk? He never failed to disconcert her, no matter how well she had prepared to face him! The words burst from her, "I didn't start that fire yesterday!" She was becoming paranoid! Why did she think he would accuse her of such a thing?

The pencil in his hand struck the desk top with a loud whack as he flung it down. "Did I accuse you?" His blue eyes blazed.

"No, but . . ."

"Then don't bother me with details that don't interest me. Jennifer, I called you in to tell you about a change I'm making."

Oh, heavens, she thought. *He's going to fire me. He'll send me down as soon as the big chair's running. And I asked for it.*

Suddenly Jennifer knew that more than anything she wanted to stay at the Rainbow. She swallowed twice, painfully, before he released her from his stare.

Once more she found herself staring at his bent head as he studied the papers on his desk. He said, "I want you to move in with Cassie."

"You . . . want . . . *what?*"

"You heard me. You are to gather up your things and move them into Cassie's room. Her room is larger than yours. Big enough for two. Please get it done as soon as possible."

"But that's impossible," Jennifer said.

"Nothing is impossible, Jennifer. Now get busy. I'm sure you have as much to demand your attention as I do. And please close the door behind you."

She was being dismissed. Nothing she could say, Jennifer was certain, would make Dominic Martin change his plan for this latest torture.

No wonder, she thought as she dragged herself from his office, *Cassie was in such a bad mood this morning.* Of all the members of Dominic's staff, there surely could be no more unlikely combination than Jennifer and Cassie. But Dominic had ordered the change, and that was the way it would have to be.

Chapter Eight

It was evening before Jennifer had a chance to move her possessions and her clothing into Cassie's room. Cassie had refused to make herself available or to move her belongings from drawers and closet to give Jennifer room for her own things.

At one time Jennifer considered pushing Cassie's clothes aside in the closet to make room for her clothes, but decided against it. There was enough animosity already between them; adding to it would only make living together more difficult. Besides, Jennifer was no more eager than Cassie to share the room.

But there was no time left if they expected to accomplish the move before bedtime. And both of them knew the rage they could expect from Dominic if they delayed until another day.

By that time Jennifer had grown reconciled to the plan, and she was determined to be as friendly as possible.

She carried an armload of clothing into Cassie's room, the meager supply of clothes she had brought to the Rainbow, and hung them on the rod in the large closet where Cassie had at last, grudgingly, made barely adequate room. As she turned to the chest of drawers to see which part of it would be hers, she noticed a picture standing on top of the piece of furniture. The picture showed a round-faced baby laughing into the camera.

"What a darling baby!" Jennifer cried and swung around to face Cassie. "Is it your nephew . . . niece?"

Cassie swept past her to snatch up the picture, thrusting it under the velour top she was wearing. "None of your business," she said. She flung herself down on her bed and sat cross-legged glaring at Jennifer. "Dominic may make me share my room with you, but you needn't think I'm going to share secrets with you like a couple of dumb schoolgirls."

Jennifer forced herself to go to the closet and smooth out her clothes as they hung. She needed time to quiet the angry retort that wanted to burst forth. At last she said, "Look, I didn't mean to pry into your life, Cassie. I just saw the baby's picture and I thought it was cute."

"Yeah, all babies are cute—in pictures. At least the photo doesn't stink and yell." Her lashes shielded her eyes and her voice was so low it seemed as though she spoke to herself. Then she opened her eyes and scowled at Jennifer. "Well, you'd just better not snoop around in my things, or you might get your fingers caught in a mousetrap. I can't sit here and watch you every minute, but you'll be sorry if you 'just happen to open the wrong drawer.'" The phrase was spoken in a falsetto voice of mockery.

Jennifer could keep still no longer. She said, "Now look, Cassie. I only . . ."

"Yeah." Cassie cut her off, her mouth twisted into a sneer. "You *only* everything, don't you, Miss Purity-and-Innocence. You make me sick."

Jennifer spun around and walked from the room before she could do something she would regret, something that would get her into more trouble than she was in already.

I can't do it, she thought as she marched along the hall to her own room. *I simply can't get along with that girl.*

But she had to, she knew, if she wanted to stay on at the Rainbow. And by now she knew that she did want to stay. What was more, she had begun to suspect the reason. Dominic Martin. She was falling in love with him, though why, when he obviously hated and distrusted her, she could not understand.

She wanted to prove to him that she was trustworthy. This was vitally important to her, and if doing so meant getting along with Cassie, then that was what she would have to do.

Cassie's animosity only reinforced this determination in Jennifer. She hoped that Cassie would never know how she felt about Dominic.

That night as Jennifer was brushing her hair, Cassie again flung herself down on her own bed, sitting cross-legged as she lighted a cigarette. The ribbon of smoke that rose from the glowing tip drifted directly toward Jennifer.

"You can't get away from your conscience, can you, Jennifer?" Cassie asked insolently, the smoke curling itself into her nostrils. "It bothers you, doesn't it, about the fire—" She blew a puff of smoke toward Jennifer.

Jennifer turned around to face Cassie, the hairbrush half-raised in her hand. "Are you hinting that I started that fire?" she asked coldly.

Cassie's lashes swept down to hide her eyes. Strangely enough, they actually gave her an innocent appearance. She said, her voice like soft honey, "Who, me? Of course not. Whatever gave you that idea?" She blew another smoke ring in Jennifer's direction before stubbing out her cigarette in the ashtray by her bed. Then deliberately, she turned her back to Jennifer and began to file her nails.

Jennifer decided not to take up the challenge. They both knew how the fire had really started, so what was the point of arguing about it? The best course was silence. Perhaps if she maintained her cool, they might later be able to talk about it. But not yet. Not now. There was still too much animosity between them. And perhaps, guilt, Jennifer reflected. After all, Cassie had been responsible for a near tragedy that would have endangered them all. And it probably didn't help to live with a living reminder of her folly. Jennifer's burn was still quite obviously painful. And this had undoubtedly not escaped Cassie's sharp eyes.

Sharing a room with Cassie was a strain for Jennifer

and it didn't get any easier. Jennifer took every opportunity to get into the snowy outdoors where she was able to forget that there was such a person as Cassie.

At last the big chair was once more in operation, and all the guests departed. No new guests were admitted, however, because there was so much work to be done to prepare the slopes and trails. All the lodge personnel were needed to help with the physical work of digging out after the blizzard.

"We've got to dig out from this storm before the next one comes to knock us out even flatter," Dominic said one morning. "Every day we're closed means we're losing money. According to the weather survey, there's another storm in the offing. A really wet winter."

Jennifer's burn was improving steadily, and she was able to do a certain amount of outdoor work, although she found that her arm tired more easily than it should.

She spent most of her time in her office. One day she was alone there, bent over some papers on her desk, when from the corner of her eye she saw the doorway darken. Brushing the wing of her hair back from her face with her index finger, she glanced up to find the bulk of Dominic Martin filling the opening.

"May I interrupt you for a minute?" he asked.

He seemed quite formal and more than usually polite. A mood like this for him made her apprehensive because it seemed foreign to his nature. She laid down her pen and indicated with a gesture of her hand the chair on the opposite side of her desk. "Won't you sit down?"

He didn't answer, nor did he take the chair she indicated.

Instead, he came to stand in front of her desk. With his hands thrust into his pockets, he teetered back on his heels and forward again, then jerked one hand from his pocket and ran it through his fiery hair.

She thought he looked surprised at her invitation, as anxious and uncomfortable as a schoolboy approaching the principal. Jennifer wanted to laugh at the astonishing situation, but instead she managed to be as formal as he when she smiled and said, "What can I do for you?"

"Well . . ." For an instant he hesitated, then he plunged in. "Awhile back you said you wanted to quit, to leave the Rainbow. The big chair wasn't in operation then, so you couldn't. Now it is, and you can leave . . . if you want to."

A shock ran through Jennifer, but she hoped she had been able to conceal it from him. With an effort she regained her self-control and rose to her feet. She leaned across the desk with her fingertips resting on its surface as she looked straight into his eyes. "You're firing me."

"No . . . I . . . That is . . ."

"Well, I've changed my mind about leaving. You challenged me and I'm going to prove to you I'm no quitter." Somehow, his hesitation, so unusual for Dominic, irritated her and she went on, "There are one or two other things I want to prove to you too. If you don't want me to plan the activities any longer, I'll do outside work. I can chunk snow off the roof as fast as anyone, and . . ."

"Your arm?" He managed to get the question in against the torrent of her words.

"My arm is fine." She came around from behind the desk and stood before Dominic, staring determinedly up into his eyes.

He held his ground, not stepping back as she had half expected. The nearness of him, the scent of him, almost overpowered her, but she would not be weakened by his nearness. "You don't have to pay me," she said. "In fact, what I've already earned here will go to pay for my board and room. A *private* room, that is," she added firmly.

The astonishment that showed in his face gave her satisfaction, and she went on to explain, "I'm moving out of Cassie's room and back into the one you originally assigned to me."

He put his hands on her shoulders. "Jennifer," he said, his eyes deep pools of blue holding hers. "It was for your own good I put you in with Cassie."

"My own good! You mean so that Cassie could make my life miserable, spread rumors about me. . . ."

"It was to prevent any rumors."

Jennifer stifled a small gasp. Could this be true? She yearned to believe that he cared about her more than he did about Cassie. For a moment she hovered on the brink of accepting what he said, of interpreting it as she longed to do. But then she forced herself to see the other side of the picture. It was Jennifer he wanted supervised, chaperoned, not Cassie. And on more than one occasion he had given Cassie preferential treatment, whereas he was exacting and demanding of perfection in Jennifer.

Stiffening her spine, she continued her tirade, "And you can give Cassie this office, the way she's been wanting you to do. And the job with it. From now on I'm spending all my days outside, working with the crew to get the Rainbow ready for guests again. I'm not quitting, but I'm not going to be used by you any longer!"

Without waiting to see his reaction, she walked briskly out the door, shutting it firmly behind her.

Back in her room, she gathered up her few possessions and carried them to the room she had originally been assigned. That job finished, she dusted her hands, satisfied that she had stood her ground and there would be no more nonsense about rooming with Cassie.

She had fully expected Dominic to follow her, to argue with her, perhaps even to threaten her. When she had rearranged her room to suit herself and he still had not come, Jennifer began to grow anxious and uncertain. Had her actions infuriated Dominic Martin? Would he allow her to get away with such bold defiance? After all, he wasn't called The Man for nothing. Everyone here was a little afraid of rousing his temper, although no one admitted it. Yet here was Jennifer, the newest employee, boldly defying him.

Now she really had messed up her future she reflected. Paying her own way here would use up all the money she had earned, and in the end she would have no job, probably not even a recommendation.

"Jennifer," she told herself, "you are a fool with an ungovernable temper that is supposed to go with flaming hair."

Flaming hair and sapphire blue eyes! Oh, why did she ever have to meet such a man as Dominic Martin!

She could faintly hear Dominic's Huskies howling and yelping. Was he maneuvering his ungainly sled around a curve, driving them to even greater speed, his eyes as fathomless as the darkening sky, his bare head aflame under the setting sun?

Jennifer was too heartsick to go to dinner that evening. She locked her door and kept to her room all evening. Surely, she thought, someone would come to inquire why she was not helping in the cooperative effort of preparing the meal.

But no one came, and she went to bed early, but did not fall asleep until much later. Dominic's indifference had hurt her more than the expected anger.

She slept fitfully that night. In the morning she hurried outside as soon as she could to exhaust herself working in the snow.

New storm clouds were gathering. Dominic drove his crew hard. They had to clear away as much snow as possible before new flakes fell. During the night a light snow had covered some of their work. Now they had to begin again diligently clearing snow from the loading platforms of the chair lifts.

Dominic worked along with his crew, going from job to job, doing more than his share. Whether Jennifer was chunking snow off a shed's low roof, or on her skis helping to pack one of the downhill slopes, she often found him working beside her. He never mentioned her explosive outburst. In fact, he treated her as he treated any of his employees, with courtesy and kindness.

By now Jennifer had become familiar, though not expert, with both downhill and cross-country skiing. She found that she preferred cross-country to downhill. Now and then she caught Dominic watching the way she handled the long slender boards. Occasionally, he impersonally offered her a bit of advice. "Plant your pole closer to your body, like this. Gives you more push when you need it."

The advice was helpful, but Dominic's demonstrations disconcerted her, for he invariably put his arm around her to guide her. Just being near him, even working side by side with him, threw her coordination off.

Once when he grasped her shoulders, to show her the body position to take, she shivered. Through the thickness of his heavy gloves and her clothing she could feel the electricity of his touch. For an instant her breath caught in her throat. The eyes meeting hers were the warm blue of Sapphire Lake under summer sunlight.

His grip tightened on her shoulders until the pressure hurt. She would have lost her balance and fallen over into the deep snow if he had not steadied her.

"You okay now?" he asked.

Her laugh was a little shaky. "Yes. Thanks."

He left her, gliding smoothly across the slope they had been packing. She stood staring at his retreating back. Was he as affected by her nearness as she was by his? He didn't so much as glance back over his shoulder, and the blue back of his jacket told her nothing. The tight fit of his dark ski pants outlined the ripple of the flexing thigh muscles, tensing and relaxing with each thrust of his skis. Jennifer turned away, suppressing a sigh. Dominic had only been courteous to her. He would have done the same for any of the guests. He didn't even really like her. He had shown that often enough.

Jennifer worked until the increasing chill of evening began to stiffen her hands. The sun had dipped behind the rim of peaks that formed a backdrop for the lodge. Darkness came earlier to Rainbow Ridge with its screen of mountains than it did in more open areas. One by one the workers returned to the lodge.

Jennifer went directly to the fireplace where she removed her wet and half frozen gloves to warm her hands before the blaze.

Cassie lay directly in front of the fireplace. She was dressed in a bright red jump suit of a soft material that rippled with each movement of her voluptuous body and clung to the curve of her hips. The neckline was slit low. It was an after-ski outfit meant only for lounging and not for outdoor wear. She was reading a book and music blared from a tape recorder on the floor beside her. It was obvious that she had not been helping with the outside work.

Before she thought, Jennifer said, "I see you weren't outside doing your share of the work."

Cassie's long lashes flickered up as she swept Jennifer with a glance. "Why should I get my hands all red and ugly with work?"

Jennifer involuntarily glanced at her own hands. "The rest of us do it," she replied impatiently.

Cassie's grin was twisted. "So I see."

Although Jennifer knew she would get nowhere

arguing with Cassie, she could not stop herself. She said, "It helps Dominic and it helps the Rainbow."

Slowly, like a cat stretching, Cassie rose to her feet. "I help Dominic . . . in other ways." The unbelievable eyelashes fluttered demurely down to shield her eyes.

As Jennifer stood numb, trying desperately to think of a suitable reply, Cassie said, "If you must know, Dominic and I are engaged to be married."

If she had hit Jennifer with her fist, the blow could not have been more staggering. Jennifer stood dumbfounded, while Cassie moved away, her hips swaying provocatively, to make the full legs of her jumpsuit ripple around her body.

It can't be true, Jennifer told herself. Cassie has lied before. She must be lying now.

Cassie turned back to say over her shoulder, "Dominic's taking me down to the village the very first day he has time. To pick out a ring. An engagement ring."

Then it must be true! And now Jennifer realized how hopeless her own love for Dominic was. Although she had suspected he was in love with Cassie, she had nevertheless held onto a spark of hope that someday, somehow, he would discover what an unpleasant person she was. Then, in Jennifer's fantasies, he would drop Cassie and turn to her.

But this was not to be. She went with heavy heart to help with the preparation for the evening meal.

That night Dominic warned them of the avalanche danger. "There's a cornice that's about ready to break off up there above the Starshoot run. I want Nick to go up there first thing in the morning and blast it before it does any damage. And there may be others just as bad." He assigned members of his maintenance crew to check the other ski slopes. "But don't do anything except observe until you talk it over with me. I had promised Cassie I'd go down to the village with her tomorrow, but there's a group of musicians coming up and I've got to talk to them. If they sound as good up here as they did when I heard them in Tahoe, we'll have music to dance by every evening."

The others shouted with enthusiasm, but Jennifer had heard only his first announcement, and her spirits sank. Dominic had promised to take Cassie down to the village as soon as he could. This confirmed what Cassie said about selecting her ring. They must really be engaged.

For the remainder of that day she went about her duties with the automatic motions of a robot, her thoughts on the depressing news she had heard.

After dinner Jennifer listlessly scraped plates in the kitchen to prepare them for the dishwasher while the other staff members brought their own plates in to her.

Most of the staff had a teasing word or a joke for her as they came in, but she noticed a strange and ominous silence as the ski instructors, one by one, brought in their plates and set them down. *Surely,* Jennifer thought, *Cassie's news, confirmed by Dominic, couldn't have had anything to do with their suddenly unfriendly manner, could it?*

Linc was the last to bring in his plate. As she knew him the best she decided to ask, "What have I done to freeze them up, Linc?"

Linc avoided her eyes. "Look, Jennifer, why don't I get the gang together in here to tell you what they're mad about. They owe it to you to let you know so you can change your attitude," he said awkwardly.

"Change my attitude! What's wrong with my attitude, Linc?"

But already he had left the kitchen.

In a short time he was back with the others. Linc said, "I had to agree to be the spokesman, Jennifer, but I want you to know I still like you in spite of everything."

Jennifer jerked her hands out of the water, flinging drops in all directions, as she spun around to face them. "In spite of everything!" she echoed. "Look, just tell me what you're mad about, *please!*"

"Well, it's what you said about all us instructors," Linc said, looking as if he hated what he had to do.

Jennifer drew her brows together to stare from one to another. Without smiling, they nodded their agreement. "And just what am I supposed to have said?" she asked.

"That none of us were good enough to teach kindergarten kids to ski."

"I said no such thing!" Jennifer protested. "It's about as far from what I think as . . ."

She got no further, with each one interrupting, speaking loud enough to be heard above the others while Jennifer also shouted to be heard. The kitchen became a bedlam of sound.

Linc laid a protective arm across her shoulders as he tried to outshout the others.

At that instant the door from the main part of the lodge opened and Dominic stood in the doorway, his eyes steel hard, flicking from one person to the other.

Jennifer broke away from Linc's friendly and protective embrace, but not, she saw, before Dominic's glance caught the two of them in its sharp focus.

Into the instant silence that enveloped the room at his entrance, Dominic Martin said, "From the sound of things before I opened the door, Jennifer, I assumed you were embroiled in another mess, and I came in to help. But I can see now it's only a lovers' quarrel, so I'll leave you to straighten it out yourself. I've important things to do before I go to the village tomorrow."

"But I . . ." Jennifer began, but it was too late. Dominic had left the room.

As if he took the silence with him, his departure was followed by a return of the pandemonium. The ski instructors all tried to outshout each other.

Jennifer said, "He misinterprets everything I do or say." Her voice was so soft in the hubbub that she had not expected to be overheard.

But they had overheard, perhaps because of the sharp contrast between their shouts and her quiet voice. And it turned the tide of their feelings.

"The Man can't talk that way to you!" someone shouted. "We . . . we won't let him!"

"It's all Cassie's fault. She started the rumor."

"We ought to know better than to believe her by now," Linc said. "Let's go tell The Man Cassie lied about Jennifer."

Jennifer grabbed his arm. "No!" she cried. It was too late for that. The damage had already been done, and Dominic would side with Cassie. He'd have to, since he was going to marry her. Jennifer pulled herself together. "I'm really grateful to you guys for taking my part, and I'm glad you realize now that I didn't run you down the way Cassie said I did. You're all great skiers and great teachers. You taught me to ski, didn't you?" With a laugh that wasn't as lighthearted as she wished it had been, she added, "And look what a top-notch skier I am!"

In unison they shouted, "Yaa, Jennifer! She's *numero uno!*"

When they had quieted at last, Jennifer said, "It won't do any good to go to Dominic. He's . . . well . . . Just do me a favor and forget it, will you?" She couldn't bring herself to tell them that Dominic was engaged to Cassie.

"Sure, Jennifer," they agreed. They would do as she asked, but they could not understand why she asked it.

And she could never tell them.

Chapter Nine

Dominic's meeting with the new band apparently was successful, for the next evening everyone gathered in the main lounge to be treated to an evening of dancing. All the employees of the lodge were there, and Dominic seemed to be in an especially good mood as he joined them.

Perhaps it was the resolving of the differences between the ski instructors and Jennifer that gave those volatile athletes an added zest that evening, but Jennifer found herself in great demand as a dancing partner for the various members of the team of instructors as well as the other men.

The band, although small, produced lively music that seemed to set the walls of the lodge to vibrating. It also had such good rhythm that standing still was almost impossible. The musicians, playing a guitar, a clarinet and an electronic organ that included symbols and drums, appeared to enjoy performing as much as the others enjoyed dancing.

Jennifer liked dancing with the instructors, all of whom had superb senses of rhythm, grace and balance, with each using his own style to express his skill. But the evening had overtones of misery and unhappiness for her.

As usual, Cassie added a disturbing note. Wearing her favorite crimson, she was a moving flame as she danced. Her costume tonight was a gown with a floor length skirt of chiffon cut so generously that it billowed about her legs while it clung to her hips, outlining their seductive roundness. The bodice of the dress was a shirred bandeau that bound her full breasts while at the same time it displayed with emphasis the deep cleavage between them. As her bare, creamy shoulders moved, the restraining cloth moved lower exposing even more her full breasts.

Jennifer had chosen a full skirt of green quilted cotton that she felt would be appropriate in the informal setting. With it she wore a white silk blouse that contrasted with the glowing tan her face had acquired since she came to the Rainbow. She had always thought her own figure reasonably well proportioned, but now, compared with Cassie's voluptuousness, she felt positively skinny. And watching the vibrant Cassie as she posed and displayed her curves, Jennifer felt that she faded into the background, too plain, too conservative to be noticed, at least by Dominic Martin.

Linc noticed her, however. When he saw her he hurried over to join her. "Hi, gorgeous," he said with a grin. "You'll really blast the guys into orbit in that outfit, Green Eyes."

Jennifer was so pleased over the compliment, and so buoyed up after her depressed feelings, that she impulsively raised her head and kissed Linc on the cheek. "You're sweet, Linc," she said. "Even if you're lying, you've made my evening."

"I'd never lie to you, sweetheart," he said. "And you'll always be my queen, even though I have to play second fiddle to you-know-who."

Of course he was kidding, but Jennifer wondered if he had only hit on a lucky guess or if he really knew that it was Dominic she loved. As sweet as Linc was, she could never love him as she loved The Man.

Whether or not Linc meant the words, he caught Jennifer in his arms and drew her to him. "A kiss on the cheek's no way to treat a guy, Jennifer. Here's what I can do for you." His mouth came down on hers before she could pull away.

Jennifer set her fists against him and pushed with all her strength. "Linc!" she remonstrated, "you shouldn't . . ." She broke off as her glance moved as if pulled by some unknown force. To her shock she met the steady gaze of the very man who had been the focus of her thoughts. Dominic Martin himself.

How much had Dominic seen? How much had he heard? In her thoughts she reviewed the brief and inconsequential bit of talk between Linc and herself. It had meant nothing really, but would it seem so insignificant to a casual listener, to Dominic? And—

Jennifer felt her face grow warm as another thought disturbed her—worst of all, *she* had initially kissed Linc, even though it had been nothing more than a friendly brush of her lips against his cheek.

Linc had also noticed Dominic observing them, for he said, a foolish grin splitting his face, "Hey, Dominic, to the victor belongs the spoils, huh?"

Jennifer couldn't help wincing. What could have possessed Linc to make that statement, the worst thing he could have said?

"Congratulations," Dominic said and walked directly across the floor to claim Cassie for a dance.

As he gathered her into his arms, Cassie's head nestled contentedly against his chest. Jennifer could not pry her attention from them as they began to dance together. The red of Cassie's outfit clashed with the burnished tones of his hair as the soft light caught it, making Cassie's outfit look garish and theatrical. And yet Jennifer had to admit that the two made a striking pair in a dance that was more sensual than Jennifer liked to see. She turned away.

Linc said, "Sorry, Jennifer, I don't know why I said a dumbfool thing like that. I know you really go for The Man, and I wouldn't mess things up between you two for anything, even though it means cutting my own throat. Maybe there's something I can say that will make things better, huh?"

"No, Linc, let well enough alone. Please. There's really nothing between Dominic and me anyway, so don't worry. But just don't put on a show for everyone again, okay?" She squeezed his hand and smiled up at him to take some of the sting out of her words, but still let him know she disliked his taking advantage of her friendliness the way he had.

"Okay, you're the boss. Next time I'll settle for a chaste buss on the cheek."

Next time, Jennifer thought, *I'll know better than to let my vanity run away with me.* She would find some other way of showing her appreciation for Linc's friendship.

She may have felt her outfit that evening was too conservative, but apparently the men did not, for Jennifer did not lack for partners all evening. More often than not, she found that her dancing partner was Linc, but there were plenty of others as well. It seemed that as soon as one of the other men claimed her for a dance and took her away from Linc, he returned to dance the next number with her. At first Jennifer enjoyed this, for Linc seemed to be the one whose dancing she found easiest to follow. Moreover, Linc was easy to talk to. Jennifer knew she could never feel anything other than friendship for him, but between the two of them there was a warm camaraderie that gave Jennifer a comfortable, relaxed feeling.

While she was dancing with Linc, they happened to move close to Dominic and Cassie who were dancing together, his head bent close over hers while hers was tipped back and she looked up at him, her eyes liquid and framed by her lashes.

Jennifer felt her own muscles tense with dislike, and she made a great effort to relax so that she would not miss a step or give Linc any hint of the turmoil that was going on in her thoughts.

As they brushed past the other couple, both men by chance swung their partners around in such a way that all four seemed to form a nucleus surrounded by the other dancers.

In those minutes when they were so close, Jennifer overheard a few words spoken between Cassie and Dominic.

Cassie said, "I just don't know Dominic. Marriage is a serious business. Do you really think I'll be able to stick it out?"

"Of course you will, Cassie." Dominic's voice was strong with certainty. "I won't hear of your backing out now. You know how I've counted on it, and you know also that when I make up my mind to a thing I just don't give up."

"Oh, Dominic," Cassie cooed as she gave him one last soulful look then rested her head against his chest. "You have such faith in me. What would I ever do if I hadn't found you? I just couldn't live without your love." Jennifer heard her sigh.

"Well, you don't have to worry. I . . ." A blast of the cymbals cut off the remainder of his sentence, and at that both Dominic and Linc swung their partners away to avoid another couple whose frantic gyrations threatened to make them collide with anything in their path.

Jennifer was so upset by what she had heard that she missed a step, and Linc tightened his grasp on her to keep her in balance as he swung her out of the way of the whirling couple.

The accident avoided, Linc held Jennifer away to give her a questioning look. "You tired?" he asked.

"Oh, no. It's just . . . Well, I just caught my heel on something, I guess."

Linc gave her a dubious look, but at that moment the band leader announced that they would offer the first of a series of specialty dances, and Linc let the matter drop as they stood hand in hand to listen to the announcement from the band leader.

"Since we'll soon have families coming up and a wide age variety here," the leader said, "we've decided to intersperse some of the older types of dances we're always getting requests for, along with today's music."

There was clapping and cheering, and when it had died down at last he suggested that the first would be a square dance number. "That is, if we can find a caller. Is there anyone here who's able or willing to call for the dancers?"

His request met silence at first, and then a low groan of disappointment rose and someone said, "I've done some square dancing, but I couldn't call." A murmur of agreement followed as others admitted to familiarity with the steps, but no one was willing to attempt calling.

The band leader said, "We've a script for one of the numbers, if someone would be willing to read it in time to the music."

Again there was a silence until, to Jennifer's surprise, Linc spoke up. "I happen to know that our host, Dominic Martin, has done enough square dancing to be familiar with the terms. And he's got a good strong voice. We're all familiar with that voice of authority." After a burst of general laughter, Linc went on, "How about it, Dominic? You willing to risk it, to try your hand, or your voice, and save the evening?"

"Sure," Dominic said, grinning. "I thought I'd tried just about everything in this life, but calling a square dance will be a new experience to add to my collection.

If you're willing to put up with my lack of experience, I'll try it."

There was loud applause, and Cassie stood on tiptoe to fling her arms about his neck and put her lips up for his kiss.

Jennifer turned away so that she would not have to endure the torture of seeing Dominic kiss her rival, the successful captor of his affections.

With his easy stride he crossed the dance floor and took his place in front of the band, with the sheet of paper the musician handed him held up to prompt him. The spotlight set his hair aflame and brought out the strong lines of his face. Jennifer thought he had never appeared more compelling, but then, she told herself, *she had thought that about him in each different setting. Why*, she asked herself, *must I waste my love on someone who is so obviously tied up already with another woman?* There was no sensible answer.

Dominic proved to be as good at calling the square dance as he seemed to be at everything he attempted. His voice was strong and sure, his enunciation clear, and he kept the rhythm lively and distinct. Almost everyone joined in, although some groups showed near-professional skill while others enjoyed their own ridiculous awkwardness, laughing so hard when they became hopelessly entangled in each other that they caused some equally unskilled performers to drop out just to watch the antics of the other groups.

Jennifer and Linc joined two other employees of the lodge to make a square that was somewhere between the best and the worst. She had done some square dancing, but she was far from skilled, and she was kept busy following the fast-moving figures that Dominic ordered them to make. She caught an occasional glimpse of Dominic, however, and each time she was certain he watched her. Did he think she was woefully awkward? She missed a step and Linc had to guide her over the mistake.

While Dominic called the steps, Cassie came to stand behind him to become a self-appointed rhythm keeper. With her arms extended and her body swaying, she marked the rhythmic beat of the music. Out of the corner of Jennifer's eye she noticed that Cassie had managed to position herself so that she would be within Dominic's line of vision. She swung first to face the dancers and then around so that she faced Dominic, trying to get him to move with her. Her skirt moved with the sinuous motions of her body, and the lift of her arms threatened to dislodge her breasts from their confinement.

Although normally Jennifer enjoyed any kind of dancing, now she was thankful when at last the lively music ceased. Along with most of the others, gasping for breath after the exercise, she went with Linc to a seat away from the dance floor.

Wine flowed freely for the thirsty people gathered, and in a short time almost everyone was ready for more dancing. Now, however, they preferred a slower and less physically exhausting dance, and the band took this opportunity to fill a request for a waltz.

As the romantic strains began, Jennifer involuntarily glanced around, looking for Dominic. Not that she expected him to seek her out for any dance. He would be too tied up with his fiancée. But Jennifer could not help torturing herself with the remembered sight of him dancing with Cassie, their heads close together and their lips moving as they murmured love words to each other.

But as she looked around she was surprised to find that neither Cassie nor Dominic was anywhere around. This fact gave Jennifer's heart a new wrench, one that was even greater than the picture she had drawn in her imagination. No doubt Dominic and Cassie were off together in some secluded corner, kissing and whispering their love to each other.

She and Linc were sitting together beside the fireplace. Jennifer's wine glass, still half full, had been set on the bricks of the hearth, but Linc kept his glass in his hand, and no more than a few seconds passed without his lifting it to his lips and taking a swallow. The carafe of wine he had brought from the bar was close beside him on the floor, and it was almost empty. Jennifer knew it was not the first carafe he had purchased for the two of them, and she had lost count of how many he had bought, but she knew that her own half empty glass was only her second, and that it would probably be her last one.

Linc did not appear to be drunk, but he had been claiming more of her time. While Jennifer was fond of Linc, she wanted no one to monopolize her. In a place like this, where everyone was more or less confined in a relatively small space, and where everyone's actions were easily observed, it took little to start talk. Cassie would like nothing better than to start a rumor about Jennifer and Linc.

He was talking to her now, telling her some amusing

story about an incident from his past. But it was a lengthy account, and Jennifer had let her thoughts wander. She was wondering how she could manage to slip away from Linc without hurting his feelings. She was too deeply involved in her thoughts so when the voice spoke from close beside her she was startled.

"Why so pensive, Jennifer?" Dominic's deep tones asked.

Jennifer swung around to find herself staring into those incredibly blue eyes. "Oh, hello, Dominic. I was . . . just watching the dancers while I listened to Linc."

Dominic's left eyebrow rose as if to question her statement, but before he could speak Linc groaned and mumbled, "I might have known I couldn't hold my favorite girl's attention when The Man comes around. Hullo, Dominic." His greeting was pointedly unenthusiastic.

"If I'm interrupting something . . ." Dominic began.

"Oh, no," Jennifer said quickly. Too quickly, she realized as she saw Linc's face fall. She added, "That is, I think Linc ought to mix with the other girls. They've been giving me bad looks for monopolizing him." Then, to her horror she realized that sounded as if she expected Dominic to dance with her. He might only have come to say something to Linc. In one further attempt to right her wrong, she said, "Won't you join us, Dominic?"

His eyes had turned to steel. "I came to ask you to waltz with me Jennifer. But if you don't want to leave Linc . . ."

I've done it again, she thought. *The more I say, the worse it gets.* But already her tongue had taken over, and she heard herself say, "I'd love to dance with you, Dominic."

He bent his head to look down at Linc who still sat on the floor beside the fireplace. "Okay with you, Linc?"

"Sure," Linc said. "I'll just sit here and drown my sorrows in the fruit of the vine." He raised his glass and drained it.

Jennifer frowned at him. She wanted to caution him to go more slowly on the wine, but that would embarrass Linc with Dominic close enough to overhear, and it might make Dominic think she had more than a friendly interest in Linc. She rose to her feet and went with Dominic to the dance floor.

As Dominic caught her to him, Jennifer's heart set up such a thumping that she was certain he could feel its vibration. *I must not let him know how the warmth of him against me sets me to trembling inside,* she thought.

He held her close, and her head seemed to fit perfectly against his muscular chest. Since he was so much taller than she, Jennifer had to turn her head to the side in order to breathe. With her ear pressed against his chest she could hear the steady rhythm of his heartbeat. *Had it quickened the way her own had?* she wondered. But there was no way to tell.

Dominic's waltzing was superb. He dipped and swayed, swung her around and back again, then bending her so that she arched her back while he leaned forward over her, his face so close to hers that she was drowned in his sapphire eyes. For an instant she thought his lips would meet hers in a kiss, and she yearned toward him. But quickly and smoothly he lifted her shoulders to swing her around in another half circle.

The music swirled around them, spinning Jennifer in a whirlpool of conflicting emotions. Oh, Dominic, her heart cried out, I could waltz like this with you forever.

All too soon the number ended, and Dominic led Jennifer off the floor. He kept her hand in his, for which Jennifer was grateful. She thought she could never have managed to walk steadily without his strong support.

As they walked he said, "You're a good dancer, Jennifer."

She murmured, "Thank you. You're easy to follow." She thought she would cherish his compliment for the rest of her life, a lonely life without Dominic while he would be married to Cassie, the girl of his choice.

Dominic returned her to the same place he had found her, beside the fireplace. Linc was still sitting there, this time with a fresh carafe of wine.

"Here's your girl, Linc," Dominic said. "None the worse for having danced with me."

From Linc's place on the floor, he looked up at Dominic and said, smiling crookedly, "Are you sure she's my girl, Dominic? From the way that you two danced I could have sworn—"

Glaring at him, Jennifer interrupted quickly. "Thank you Dominic for the dance. I enjoyed it. And for your information I am not Linc's girl. Or anyone elses. We are just good friends."

"The best of friends!" Linc winked suggestively as he raised his glass.

"Yes," Dominic said. "I'm sure. Now if you'll excuse me, please . . ." Without completing the thought, he walked away.

As soon as Dominic was out of hearing range, Jennifer sank down onto the floor beside Linc and said,

"Linc! How could you! The way you talked about our friendship made it sound as if there's something more to it than there really is!"

"Well, pussycat, it's not my fault there isn't." He made a lunge for her and drew her close. As his hands fumbled for her breasts he said loudly, "How about you and me going to bed together, huh?"

As if some devilish force had planned it, the instant he spoke, the music ceased. Linc's voice reverberated through the room.

Someone chuckled, but Jennifer saw nothing amusing in the incident. She felt heat flame in her face and she jerked away from Linc. His fumbling fingers had already found the middle buttons of her blouse.

"Linc! You're drunk!" Jennifer whispered.

"No, I'm just elated," he said. "It's what you do to me, sweetheart."

Jennifer said, "I'm not going to stay with you another minute." Quickly she buttoned her blouse. "I'll come back when you can behave like a gentleman, but not before." She stood and turned to flee from him only to meet the steady gaze of Dominic Martin from across the room. A grinning Cassie clung to his arm. Jennifer opened her mouth to repute their all too obvious suspicions, but in that instant Dominic bent his head to say something to Cassie and the two turned away.

What could I have said anyway? Jennifer asked herself silently. Both Dominic and Cassie had seen the pass Linc made. They had heard his embarrassing words, made at the unfortunate time when there had been the only pause in the loud music. What was more, they probably had no idea of how much wine Linc had drunk or how he was affected by it.

Even if Dominic had been aware of all this, Jennifer was certain that Cassie would plant more suspicions in his mind. And of course he would believe Cassie. After all, he was in love with her.

Jennifer wanted nothing more than to escape from this room, the scene of her embarrassment. She rose to her feet and bent to pick up the partially emptied wine carafe from beside Linc. "You've had enough of this, Linc. I'll take it away from you."

Linc's eyes were dull as he watched her pick up the container. He made no protest as Jennifer took it to the kitchen.

The kitchen was deserted, and, as the door swung closed behind her, it was quiet. *Blessedly quiet,* Jennifer thought, for the beat of the music seemed to echo the words Linc had spoken as she had tried to ward off his fumbling hands. She had felt as if the band's spotlight was focused on her and that everyone had watched the embarrassing scene. Worst of all, that Dominic's disapproving eyes had seen and misinterpreted.

How will I ever live down the humiliation? she thought.

From outside, softly at first but with a sound that swelled on the wind, came the howl of Dominic's dogs. Carried on the night air, it was a sound of desperate loneliness. At the same time it stirred something within Jennifer as she thought of Dominic, showing encouragement to his dogs as he ran behind the sled. Jennifer leaned her arm against the door of a high cupboard, her elbow bent, and rested her head against her arm, letting it cover her eyes.

"Oh, Dominic," she whispered softly into the quiet room. "Why can't I stop loving you?"

Quickly she pushed herself away from the cabinet and lifting her chin drew in her breath sharply and deeply in her struggle to regain control of herself. There was no use in her cowering back here and feeling sorry for herself. She would walk out calmly and go to her own room, ignoring the knowing amused looks of the crowd.

When she emerged into the main lounge she saw that Linc had risen to his feet and was heading, rather unsteadily, toward the corridor that led to the bedrooms. The wine had made him sleepy, and he would undoubtedly go to bed and sleep off its effects.

How could she leave the party now? If she were to go to her own room now she would only be giving Cassie more material for further rumors. Cassie would not let anyone believe that Jennifer and Linc had gone to their respective rooms. For that matter, who would want to believe that after the suggestion everyone had overheard Linc make?

There was no choice for her. She would have to stay up, in plain sight of the others, until the last person had left the lounge that night. At least by showing that she had not left with Linc she would have more chance of overcoming the gossip caused by his unfortunate remark. With a sigh of resignation, she went into the lounge to join the remaining ski instructors there.

The next specialty was the Mexican Hat Dance. The band leader tossed a wide-brimmed straw hat into the center of the floor to form a hub around which the others would dance. Most of the people were familiar with the dance and knew the steps. Those who knew them helped others in what proved to be a very simple group dance.

The dancers formed a single circle, and with arms linked executed the bouncing motions of the first segment of the dance. Then, at a change of the tempo, they broke apart into couples, each swinging in a small circle as all moved in the general clockwise direction of the main circle. It was a spirited dance, and it put everyone into a lively mood. By the time the music had ended, even the athletic ski instructors were breathing heavily.

Jennifer had joined at the urging of the instructors who remained after Linc left. It seemed to her that they were trying to keep her amused in his absence. She was tempted to resent the fact that they tended to pair her off with Linc. On the other hand, it was far better than sitting alone by the fire, a prey to Cassie's jibes.

This dance was followed by more round dancing, which in its own way was almost as strenuous as the specialty dance had been, for the band played everything from jitterbug to disco.

To her surprise Dominic claimed another dance with her. As they moved and turned, he said, "Isn't this band the greatest? The most versatile I've heard in a long time. Just what we need for the family groups we get up here for skiing."

Jennifer agreed. "This band should please all ages."

Their impersonal discussion, however, was short-lived, and Dominic's next words made Jennifer stiffen. He said, "Isn't your boyfriend getting impatient?"

For an instant Jennifer did not understand his meaning, but the twist of his lips was unpleasant and his eyes were opaque. She said, "What boyfriend?"

"You can keep more than one satisfied on that level?"

Now she knew exactly what he referred to. It was the embarrassing scene to which Linc had subjected her earlier in the evening. Dominic thought she had encouraged Linc. Now he was hinting that Linc must be waiting for her to join him in bed.

Well, she thought, *I'll not let him know I understand his reference!* She met his gaze squarely as she said, "I've no idea what you mean."

"Linc's disappeared. Isn't he waiting for you?"

"Linc had too much wine, and you're a brute who hasn't the decency to try to understand." Jennifer had ceased dancing, and she stood in the midst of the other dancers, glaring at Dominic. Abruptly she realized that she was making a spectacle of herself again for people were turning to stare at her. She knew that if she remained facing Dominic Martin for one second longer she would lash out at him with worse accusations. She turned and strode from the dance floor.

She went to the fireplace and stood before it with her back to the dance floor, hoping the flush she knew reddened her face could be blamed on the heat from the blazing logs.

She hadn't stood there for more than half a minute when she heard Cassie's voice from close behind her. "What's the matter, Jennifer, did you find the heat from dancing with Dominic too much for you so you had to come cool off by the fire?" Cassie's voice had been no more than a soft purr, but her enunciation was precise, and Jennifer could not fail to understand. The question was followed by Cassie's usual high-pitched laugh.

Jennifer was determined not to give Cassie the satisfaction of knowing her remark had stung. Showing no sign she had heard, she continued staring into the fire. Cassie moved away.

It was only a short time later that the band leader's announcement brought Jennifer out of her reverie.

"We have a very special treat," the leader said. "Fulfilling a personal request, our next number will be a solo. There was a fanfare from the band, and he went on, louder than before, "May I present the indomitable Cassandra!"

Jennifer whirled around to face the dance floor. A spotlight struck Cassie's undulating crimson outfit as she stood in triumph, accepting the applause.

Shouts, wolfcalls and thundering applause set the smiling Cassie in motion as she began to remove first the red skirt and then she unzipped the bandeau to reveal a few scraps of purple silk and gold chains from which dangled coins of gold. She gathered up the red outfit and tossed it from the floor where someone caught it. She kicked off her sandals as she began to sway and undulate in time with the music.

Cassie's act was of professional quality. Arms extended, she swayed her shoulders suggestively. She moved her hips, one at a time, to set the gold coins jingling in the same rhythm as the music. She seemed able to control muscles Jennifer doubted her own body possessed. But Cassie made these odd muscles quiver along her abdomen, atop her breasts, and as she turned her back to the audience, even across her buttocks.

There was wild whistling and hooting among the men. Cassie appeared to be inspired by their excitement, for her motions became more seductive, and the gold chains tinkled as they struck each other in their swaying rhythm.

Jennifer could not deny that Cassie had an alluring body. *But it isn't fair,* she thought, *for her to use it to capture Dominic!*

She glanced around the audience, searching for him, hoping to see some hint of disapproval in his expression. All around her there was a sea of eager faces and grinning men. Jennifer thought, *All she has is a body. There's nothing else about her that's real. Can't they see that?*

But no matter how she searched through those fascinated watchers, she could not find Dominic. Maybe he was unaware of the spectacle Cassie was making of herself. Would he find it attractive? Had he left in disgust? She could no longer deny to herself that this last thought gave her a guilty pleasure. Shameful as it was, she had to recognize that she was *jealous.* Jealous that Cassie had Dominic's love that she longed to capture for herself.

She picked up her all-but-forgotten glass of wine and stared into it, wondering if Linc's way of finding oblivion in the wine might be helpful. *No,* she answered her question. That would be a coward's way out. Besides, sooner or later she would have to face the future without Dominic. She might as well start with a clear head.

Before she could set the wine glass down Jennifer noticed a commotion nearby. Cassie's number had come to its end, and as Cassie sank down in a bow that acknowledged the applause, her red costume was being handed from one of the ski instructors to another. Jennifer heard one of them say, "Keep it away from her. She looks good this way!"

Suddenly the red outfit was thrust at Jennifer. "Hide

it for us, Jennifer. She'll never suspect you have it," the instructor said.

His aim was accurate, but he must have underestimated his own strength, for the bundle of folded red cloth sailed through the air to strike Jennifer full on, unfolding as it struck her, enveloping her in the red silky material.

The force of the blow was enough to spill the wine from the glass she held in her hand, and by the time Jennifer had extricated herself from the cloth, much of it had been soaked in wine.

Cassie, now apparently aware of the fate of her outfit, came striding across the floor to confront Jennifer.

When she stood facing her, her fists jammed on her hips, she glared at Jennifer and cried, "You've ruined my new outfit! How dare you!" Her hand was raised as though to slap Jennifer.

Before Jennifer could reply, Dominic appeared from somewhere and caught Cassie gently by her bare shoulders to swing her around to face him. "Cassie, dear, don't make such a fuss about a dress that can easily be replaced if it can't be cleaned," he said with gentleness that astonished Jennifer.

How could he be so gentle with this female cat, she thought, when her own slightest misdemeanor drew his cutting anger?

The answer was obvious. *Dominic loved Cassie.* He despised Jennifer. She closed her eyes so that she couldn't see his hands on Cassie's bare flesh.

Dominic had been successful in calming Cassie. She looked up at him, blinking her eyes to display the long lashes, and said in the pouting manner of a spoiled child, "Then you'll buy me a new outfit to replace the one Jennifer ruined, Dominic?"

"Yes, Cassie. We'll go down to the village tomorrow. But come now, it's bedtime for you and for all the rest of us. We've a big day ahead tomorrow."

As he led her away, Cassie turned back to give Jennifer a wink that set her temper blazing. Tomorrow Dominic and Cassie would go down to the village, and not only would they buy her a new outfit, but they would select an engagement ring. *I can't bear it,* Jennifer thought as she made her way to her room.

Before she reached her room, another thought, still more depressing, came to her. *Dominic and Cassie had gone toward the bedroom wing together. Would they end up in the same bed?*

As she lay in her lonely bed, tears stung behind her eyes. From outside, suddenly came the sound of Dominic's dogs howling, baying into the night, calling him as Jennifer longed to call him.

She flung herself over and buried her head in her pillow allowing her tears to flow unchecked.

Chapter Ten

Dominic and Cassie left Rainbow Lodge early the next morning, riding down together in the same double chair. Jennifer tried not to watch them as they slipped easily into the chair to sit side by side. She could not help remembering her own last ride up the mountain with Dominic just as the storm broke, when the chair had stopped midway up the mountain. She felt again a stirring of passion as she remembered the touch of his hands as he had rubbed warmth into her. She was certain that he had felt the same way. But now, seeing him with Cassie, she mistrusted her own powers to stir him. She hoped his ride down with Cassie would be speedy and uneventful.

Cassie literally sparkled that morning, with the hood of her crimson parka thrown carelessly back to allow the morning sunlight to turn her hair to glittering gold.

Her eyes glistened beneath their incredible fringe of lashes as she slanted her looks up at Dominic.

She's two-faced, Jennifer thought, *but if he can't see through her tricks, he deserves what he's getting.* Nevertheless, it hurt her to watch him falling into the trap Cassie had set for him.

Not that Dominic gave any sign of being swayed by Cassie's charm. His expression gave Jennifer no clue as to his reaction to Cassie's charms.

But not even Cassie's bright coloring could overshadow Dominic. His nondescript parka of midnight blue was a fitting background for the flame of his hair, while in the morning sunlight his eyes matched the blue of Sapphire Lake so far below. With a sigh that did not relieve the pain clutching at her heart, Jennifer turned from watching their chair descend. She hurried out to the ski slopes where she hoped to lose herself in hard physical work and erase from her mind the picture of Dominic and Cassie going off together to the village to choose an engagement ring.

She jabbed the shovel into a drift of snow that threatened to block the progress of the poma lift, scooped up a mound of the white stuff, and flung it across the slope, determined to shift her thoughts from what Dominic and Cassie might be up to in the village.

A short time later, Linc joined her. He greeted Jennifer and picked up a shovel, but he did not immediately begin to work. Instead, he said, "I guess I owe you an apology, Jennifer."

She stopped her own work to look at him, raising her eyebrows in a question, although she knew what he meant.

Linc went on, "I was plenty smashed, but I kind of

remember acting like an idiot, putting you on the spot."

"It was the wine that made you do it, Linc," she said.

He made a squirming motion with his shoulders. "Yeah, I guess so. But I'm no green kid. I ought to know when to quit. You know I'd do anything in the world for you, Jennifer. I wouldn't hurt you on purpose."

He looked so miserable that Jennifer said, "Forget it, Linc. We all make mistakes. Why don't you forget work too today? You look as though you could use some more sleep."

"I sure could, Jennifer." He made a feeble attempt to grin. "I guess I will, since The Man's not around. But I had to come tell you how sorry I am, not that it'll do much good at this late date. You'll probably never forgive me, hollowhead that I am, but I'll make it up to you some way."

"I've already forgiven you, Linc," she said. "Now go finish your sleep."

He held her eyes with his own. "You're the greatest, Jennifer. I sure hope whoever gets you realizes how lucky he is."

She laughed. "Flatterer. Go on now before you build me up too high for my own good."

Linc jabbed his shovel into the deep snow and with a salute walked away. His step was slow, and to show her how he felt he caught his head in his hands as if he were carrying it.

Jennifer worked on throughout the morning. By noon her body was tired but her thoughts still churned around Cassie and Dominic in the village. She knew the edges of her temper were ragged as she returned to the lodge.

To her surprise, Cassie was already there, eating her lunch at the table reserved for the staff. Dominic was nowhere to be seen. There was only one vacant chair at the table, a chair next to Cassie's.

When Jennifer had filled her plate from the assembly line on the warming table, the chair was still vacant. Left no choice, Jennifer took it. As she sat down, she could not help glancing at Cassie's left hand. There was no engagement ring.

On an impulse, Jennifer said, "Where's your ring, Cassie? I thought you were going to pick it out today."

For a split second Cassie looked at her with malice, but her voice was honey-smooth when she said, "Dominic wouldn't have any of the junk they offered us. 'Nothing but the best for my little Cassie,' he said. 'We'll wait till we can go to the city and get a really nice stone.'" Cassie rose and carried her empty plate back to the kitchen.

Jennifer had received the answer to her question, but it had not satisfied her.

After lunch she returned to the outdoors where she again tried to lose herself in hard physical work. She did not see Dominic, for which she was grateful. That would have been just too much to bear, knowing that he intended to go through with his engagement and marriage to Cassie. How could he love the girl? How could he possibly love someone like Cassie?

By late afternoon the promised storm had come, bringing wind and blowing snow. Now there was no use in continuing the outdoor work. Those who had been out came inside and gathered around the open fire to dry their wet clothing and warm themselves. Still Jennifer had not seen Dominic, and she dared not ask about him for fear of revealing her own feelings. She did her best to convince herself that she cared nothing for him or what he chose to do with his future. He could marry a dozen Cassies for all she cared!

But Jennifer knew that she did care, and not all her bravado eased the misery within her.

When the evening meal was finished and the dishes had been neatly stacked, Jennifer excused herself to go to bed, pleading fatigue from the physical labors of the day. As she hurried along the corridors, she could hear the whining wind whistling around the lodge. Further off, one of Dominic's Huskies was mournfully howling.

Suddenly, she was plunged in total darkness. She stopped, exasperated and confused. Groping her way ahead of her, she tried to remember just how far along the corridor she had come. "Blast," she muttered.

Somewhere close, she heard the swish of a door being opened. Someone had stepped into the corridor. As she caught the distinctive scent of citrus and . . . was it sandalwood? . . . she knew instantly that Dominic Martin was also groping his way through the dark hallway.

She wanted to avoid him, to slip past him without giving away her presence. She couldn't confront him now, not the way she felt. But her breath, her entire body it seemed, froze into immobility. She could not move around him. She couldn't even speak out to warn him of her presence.

As she might have anticipated, he crashed into her, knocking her off-balance.

A small cry escaped from her. At almost the same instant, he caught her in his arms to keep her from falling. "Jennifer." His voice made it a soft sound, almost a caress as his lips formed her name.

The darkness, the tender way he had spoken her name, the male scent of him were too much for her. Jennifer relaxed against him, shaping her body to fit against his strength. At the same time as his arms tightened around her, her own stole up to close around him.

His kiss sent fire surging through her veins. The darkness seemed to explode into a myriad of sparkling lights.

Suddenly Jennifer remembered Cassie. No matter how she disliked and envied the girl, the fact remained that Dominic was engaged to her. He had no right to make love in the darkness to someone else!

She set her hands against his chest and thrust him from her. "You're a fraud—a deceiver—you're two-faced Dominic Martin—I despise you . . .!" The words tumbled out one after the other in such swift profusion that they seemed to run together like one long word. As they slowed to an uncertain finish the lights came on as abruptly as they had gone off, catching the two of them in the sudden glare.

Although Jennifer had pushed back from him, Dominic had not entirely released his hold on her. His hands gripped her upper arms, his fingers digging into her flesh as he glowered at her. "I don't know what that was all about, Jennifer, but I understood the tone, and I can give it back to you measure for measure. You're an uncaring, malicious tease."

Still he did not release her. The leaping of a muscle along his jaw should have warned her of how high his temper had risen. Nevertheless, she was unprepared for his next move.

With his fingers digging into the muscles of her upper arms, he bent his head and gave her a punishing kiss. His mouth demanded of hers, pressing her lips against her teeth until she tasted blood.

"Maybe that's what you want!" Roughly he flung her aside and strode away down the corridor.

Jennifer leaned weakly against the frame of a door until she could gather enough strength to move on to her room. Why had he been so angry?

He had used her for his own pleasure, she thought with indignation, stirring her senses with a kiss he had no right to give. He was engaged to Cassie! It was Dominic Martin who deserved punishment, not her!

Jennifer lay awake part of that night, trying to make a decision. On the one hand, she felt she could not stay on at the Rainbow, seeing Dominic Martin every day to be reminded of this most recent devastatingly emotional encounter between them, and knowing all the time that he would soon marry Cassie. On the other hand, Jennifer could not bear the thought of leaving the Rainbow, of never seeing Dominic again. "I hate him," she told herself as she lay in the dark softness of her bed. "He is no better than Cassie. The two deserve each other."

Yet why did her own heart lurch whenever she remembered his kisses? Why did she burn with jealous anger when she thought of Cassie receiving those kisses?

She tossed and turned until exhaustion overcame her and she slept at last.

Morning brought her no relief, although the storm had passed over and the sunlight struck sparks of silver fire from the freshly fallen snow.

At breakfast Linc came to sit beside Jennifer. "Want me to introduce you to the pure joy of skiing deep powder?" he asked her. "Nothing can match it, and there's a whole mountain of the stuff out there this morning just waiting for us to mark it with our ski tracks."

Jennifer hesitated only a moment. She had heard enough about deep powder skiing to know that it was highly prized, a condition rarely found in some parts of the country. *Maybe,* she thought, *she could lose herself in skiing deep powder, if it proved to be as enjoyable as everyone said.* And with Linc to coach her, this should be an exceptional opportunity.

She fought down her depression and smiled at him. "Sounds great to me, Linc. I'd love it."

He grinned back at her. "You look in need of some fun. The Man's been working you too hard. . . ." He broke off when she let her closed face tell him she had had enough.

Instead, he said, "Okay, get your ski things on and meet me outside the ski shop. I'll have our boards ready."

When she went to her room, she did not change from the white turtleneck jersey she had pulled on this morning, but she traded the plaid wool slacks for the green ski outfit that had been so unsuitable for her first appearance at the Rainbow. Now, while Jennifer felt her skiing ability still fell short of the promise given by the appearance of the smart jump suit and parka, at least she knew how to handle the long boards of cross-country skiing.

She took one last glance at herself in the mirror and, on impulse, added the pink hat Linc had rescued for her. She could not fully explain her reasons for wearing it, but she knew somehow that she must wear it. She took the precaution, however, of tying it on with a scarf. She did not want to risk losing it to the wind again.

There was very little wind when Jennifer and Linc started out. The sun had so warmed the air that Jennifer at first thought that she might be too warmly dressed.

But Linc wouldn't allow her time to go back and change. "It's powder we're after today," he said. "And it won't last long. At the rate that sun's going, the powder will grow an icy crust before we get halfway up the mountain. We're going to try for the summit of Lookout."

"The summit!" Jennifer echoed. "Lookout Mountain?" She tipped her head back and squinted into the brightness. The rounded summit thrust itself into the sky far above them. She tried to swallow but could not.

"Sure," Linc said. "You can do it. You're an expert now, didn't I teach you?"

His laugh was as contagious as his assurance, and Jennifer dug her poles into the snow and shoved off behind him, keeping up with his pace.

For an hour or so she enjoyed the strenuous exercise in the sparkling outdoors. They climbed steadily, and although she followed directly in the tracks Linc carved, it was hard work. Linc, breaking trail ahead of her, appeared tireless. Trickles of sweat ran down her back and between her breasts. She unzipped her parka from both top and bottom.

"Hey, Linc, where's all the joy of flying through deep powder you promised? So far, it's just hard uphill work!" she cried out.

"Wait till we start down, girl," he called back over his shoulder, pausing in his kick-glide motion to add, "It'll be one long, beautiful run down."

Jennifer didn't answer. She had to save her breath for the effort of climbing. But she was failing. She dropped farther and farther behind. Linc did not notice as he plunged on ahead.

As they came up on a wide shoulder of the mountain, with the face dropping sharply away to one side, Linc took a detour, veering in toward the wall of the mountain as it rose above them. Jennifer, stopping to rest and catch her breath, saw that he was making a wide arc. His tracks curved in toward the wall, and then back out again to continue along the edge.

She frowned as she watched. She thought it a waste of energy. A straight line would have been easier and more direct.

She felt that Linc didn't understand how limited was her strength. Intoxicated with the beauty of the morning and the vast stretches of the unbroken powder, he appeared to have forgotten all about her.

Jennifer decided that she would not waste her precious energy. She would take the more direct route. She left his tracks and moved ahead in a straight line toward the point where his tracks would again intersect her path.

Linc glanced back over his shoulder. He shouted something but a sharp report exploding beneath her feet blotted out all sound. Linc leaped up into the air, then vanished.

At the same instant Jennifer was jerked violently off-balance and hurtled into a seething mass of tumbling, boiling, churning snow and debris. A roaring filled her ears.

The cornice! Avalanche! The dread words beat in Jennifer's mind amid the chaos of sound and motion in which she was caught. She knew that Linc had curved away from a cornice of snow that hung over the edge. And she had skied straight onto it, breaking it loose!

Swim! Instinct told her. She flexed her arms and legs as best she could as she was swept along and down the mountainside. She closed her eyes tightly and held her breath, swimming with all her strength. She kept her head down, tucking her nose into the turtleneck of her jersey to keep the snow out of her nostrils.

An endless agony of motion! An endless explosion of sound! Jennifer was hurtled, jerked, plummeted with stones and branches, bounced and tossed and flung from side to side. The roar, hiss, and rush beat against her eardrums and deafened her.

After an eternity, she found her body lodged against some immovable part of the mountainside, while the avalanche and its force swept on above her.

At last it began to quiet. When all around her was still, Jennifer tried to move.

There was no question of even sitting up, much less of standing. Heavy snow above her pressed her back each time she tried. She managed to move her head back and forth, ever so slightly, to enlarge the air space around her nose. Here the ski training she had received was invaluable. She concentrated on her breathing, keeping it slow and as shallow as possible.

She could feel the cold snow around her head, so she guessed that the force of the avalanche had jerked her pink hat away. Now there was complete silence in her snowy cocoon.

She wondered if Linc had escaped. He had been far from her. Yet she had seen him catapult into the air. Where was he now?

She thought of Dominic Martin. She needed him more than ever now. Expending her precious limited supply of oxygen, with what might even be her last breath, she whispered, "I love you, Dominic Martin. With all my heart I love you." But who could hear her in that vast, white silence?

Chapter Eleven

Time lost its meaning as Jennifer lay buried in the snow. She fought down panic, straining her ears for some sound that might bring hope, but there was none. She ventured a cry, "Linc?"

No answer. It seemed to Jennifer that just that one sound escaping from her lips, made breathing more difficult. It was as if the cry had used up most of her little oxygen supply. She forced herself to take slower, more shallow, and measured breaths.

At first she was comfortably warm and did not feel the chill of the snow that surrounded her. But as time wore on and she could not move, a coldness overcame her mind as well as her body. What if no one came to dig her out? Her oxygen supply would soon be exhausted. A deathlike chill began to pervade her body. . . .

Some time later, she thought she heard the howling

and yelping of dogs. Had she imagined it? In her ice prison, she strained her ears, but all was silent again.

She dozed and lost consciousness. Some hours, or was it minutes later Jennifer thought she heard human voices.

". . . Jennifer's hat!" Was the sound real or only in her fevered imagination?

Another voice, "Unhitch the lead dog . . . trained for rescue work . . . must be near here."

Dominic's voice!

She tried to shout, "I'm here! Right here!"

"Here's a ski . . . Give the dog the hat to sniff, then let him dig between here and there. He'll know when he's on the right track."

"I'm here. . . ." But her voice trailed away. They had not heard her. The air around her face was stale. Breathing became more and more difficult. . . . Could she make her air supply last until . . . ?

A sob shook her body. She was going to die before . . . Slowly, easily, gently, like the gentle fall of myriads of snowflakes, consciousness slipped from Jennifer.

She drifted with the snow to a land where there was neither warmth nor cold. Time stood still.

"She's alive!"

A shadow dimmed the light that flooded in. Dominic bent closer to look at her. "We'll have you dug out in minutes, Jennifer. Just hang on and keep calm."

Now she could hear the furious scratching of his digging, and shortly one of his bare hands broke through just in front of her face.

Panic threatened her as she feared he would block the precious new source of air with his frantic digging.

As her body was gradually uncovered, Jennifer felt an hysterical impatience to be free. Where she had been almost reconciled to her prison of snow, resigning to her inevitable fate, now that she was near to freedom again, she could not bear the suspense.

Perhaps Dominic understood this frustration in her, for he talked as he worked. "Mikki is a wonder," he said, speaking of his rescue dog. He told her how the dog's instinct leads him to locate a person buried under the snow better than a human's logic can do. "And he's been trained to stop digging before his claws can injure the person he's rescuing."

At last Dominic had a hole large enough to bring Jennifer out. He put his hands under her shoulders and gently lifted her out and onto the blanket he had spread on the snow.

"Thanks, Dom . . . i . . . nic," she managed to say. "For saving . . ."

"Save your strength." His voice was gruff, and his hands probed her body for broken bones.

By now, reaction had set in. Jennifer trembled so that she scarcely felt the touch of his hands.

"Thank goodness there doesn't seem to be anything but shock and chill. If Cassie hadn't seen you two heading toward that shoulder before the cornice broke loose . . ." He closed his eyes, shaking his head as if to shut out the picture of what might have happened.

So it had been Cassie! She had alerted Dominic that the two were lost. Cassie had watched Jennifer and Linc make their way up the mountain. Regardless of her motives in watching them she should be given credit for reporting quickly what she had seen.

Linc! In her anguish, she had forgotten about Linc.

Now she stammered fearfully, "What about Linc? Is he . . . ?"

"I've already sent Nick with Mikki to search for him," Dominic said as he lifted her, along with the blanket, to carry her to the sled. He wrapped her in more blankets and tucked her in for the ride back to the lodge. "But I've got to get you back to a warm bed before you shake yourself to pieces."

To Jennifer, the ride back in the dogsled was but a blur of whirling whiteness. She was only dimly aware of the dogs' excited yelping, of Dominic's shouted orders to them, of the shifts in the direction of the sled as he leapt on the extended runners to maneuver it over the icy snow. Drifting in and out of consciousness, Jennifer wondered if she would ever again be truly warm and dry.

At last they reached the lodge. Without removing Jennifer's shell of blankets, Dominic lifted her from the sled and carried her through the doorway.

Jennifer had only an impression of anxious faces pressing around them. She thought she heard Dominic's repeated assurances that she was not seriously injured and that in no time Linc would be rescued, but Dominic carried her so swiftly through the corridors that she had little chance to take in more.

By the time he laid her down on a bed, however, she had regained enough of her senses to notice the colors of the spread and the draperies. Autumn colors, bold and masculine. Dominic had carried her to his own room.

Jennifer tried to struggle from him. "My . . . room," she stammered. "Not . . . yours."

"Lie still, Jennifer. Your room's a mile away. I have to get you warm in a hurry."

One of his hands held her while the other unceremoniously stripped the wet and half frozen clothing from her body. The green ski outfit was torn and dirt-streaked now, the jersey icy, as it clung to her breasts, but at least they covered her nakedness, and she clutched at them.

"Forget your modesty," he said. "You'll die of pneumonia if I don't get you dry and warm." The jersey ripped, splitting down the middle as he pulled it from her.

Her need for warmth was greater than her desire for modesty; Jennifer curled herself into a tight ball naked and shivering before him. But now Dominic seemed not even to see her nakedness, such was his anxiety over the chill that shook her.

He eased her between the sheets of his bed and pulled up the blankets. Sitting on the edge of the bed, he removed his boots. Then he removed his ski jacket and crawled in beside her, gathering her into his arms to hasten the warming of her body with the heat of his own.

As the blessed warmth began to steal over Jennifer, she relaxed against him.

For a time she lay quietly in his arms while his hands rubbed more warmth into her. But as she relaxed and warmed, his touch on her bare flesh aroused her latent desire. Along with the return of strength, came passion. Did he realize what he was doing to her?

She tried to lie still, to feign sleep, but her false body betrayed her and she began to respond to his caresses. She opened her eyes and found his waiting for her with a softness she had not expected. He moved his head and claimed her lips in a kiss.

Passion soared beyond control in Jennifer as she responded to his kiss.

A voice from the doorway shattered the spell. "So this is how you tricked him! You're bent on taking him away from me aren't you, Jennifer!" With a cry of hysterical laughter, Cassie swung away from the door and lurched down the hall.

As if Dominic had been released by a spring's uncoiling, he leaped from the bed. "Cassie! Wait!" he cried, and in his stocking feet ran across the room. "Don't go off that way!" He ran out of the room and disappeared down the hall.

Jennifer was left alone in his room, in his bed, alone with her conscience and her fury at Dominic Martin, and Cassie.

But then she remembered. *Regardless of Cassie's motives, the fact remained. Cassie had saved her life.*

What right had Dominic to make love to Jennifer when he was engaged to Cassie? And she had been a partner in his betrayal of the other woman. She did not know whom she loathed more, herself or Dominic. No matter what she thought about Cassie, she should never have come between her and Dominic. He belonged to someone else. And that someone had saved her life, no matter what her motives had been.

She could not change Dominic, but she could see that she didn't fall into the same trap. Never again would she be swept away by her attraction to Dominic! She must put temptation from her.

Jennifer swept the top sheet from the bed, wrapped it around her nakedness, and stole from the room. She hurried along the corridor, thankful to meet no one, until she reached the privacy of her own room. Thank heavens, she no longer roomed with Cassie!

Once inside, she locked the door and crept into her own bed.

Only when she had snuggled down under the covers did she realize how exhausted she was. In spite of all her troubling thoughts, she fell almost instantly into a restless sleep.

Sometime later she was roused by the rattling of the latch and a persistent knocking on her door.

"Jennifer." It was Dominic's voice, but she refused to answer. "Please open the door. I must talk to you. Please, Jennifer."

"Go away," she cried.

"Jennifer . . ."

"I hate you. I don't ever want to see you again."

Suddenly all was silence on the other side of the door.

Minutes passed. . . .

Dominic Martin had taken her at her word. He had gone away, to Cassie where he belonged. In spite of her emotional and physical exhaustion, Jennifer passed a restless, weepy night.

Next morning she felt as if every muscle, joint and bone in her body had been bruised, wrenched or torn. When she glanced in the mirror, her face appeared pale and strained. She tried on three outfits before she finally settled on a rose-colored fuzzy sweater with wool slacks in a deeper wine-red. She hoped the soft tones would give her face some color. She tied a rose colored scarf around her head partially covering her lusterless hair. She had neither the strength nor the will to shampoo it now, nor even to brush some of the highlights back into it.

When she reached the dining room, she learned that the lodge had again been opened to guests. Already there were strangers milling around.

As soon as she found one of the staff, she asked about Linc.

"Oh, he was yanked out in time. Takes more than an avalanche to do that guy in." Nick eyed Jennifer. "Matter of fact, he looked in better shape than you do. You feel like being up?"

"I'll be all right as soon as I've had breakfast," Jennifer lied. "What happened to Linc? Was he hurt?"

"Not unless you call a broken leg hurt. They took him down to the hospital."

"Oh," Jennifer said. "That's bad. Especially for a ski instructor. But it's better than what could have happened," she shuddered.

"You can say that again. An avalanche is a bad scene. Which reminds me. The Man wants to see you in his office as soon as you finish breakfast. And from the look on his face, I'd advise you not to waste any time."

Jennifer thanked him and went to the cafeteria line to choose her breakfast. But the news had driven away her appetite.

So, Dominic wanted to see her right away! He was probably angry because she had refused to talk to him last night. But now, her courage had melted like old snow. How could she face him, this morning of all mornings?

Jennifer left the breakfast line without even taking coffee. She might as well face the music at once.

She found him at his desk when she entered his office. He did not look up when she first came in and she had the opportunity to observe that he was wearing an open-throated shirt, the color of rich cream. On the pocket, she could barely make out a small but skillfully embroidered likeness of a Siberian Husky.

He lifted his gaze to measure her and she trembled, caught in the steel-gray of his accusing eyes. A small crease had formed above the high bridge of his nose, while a muscle twitched on one side of his sternly set jaw.

At last he spoke. "You look like the very devil this morning, Jennifer."

Her jaw dropped as anger flooded through her. "What do you expect? You want me to win a beauty contest after being tossed around by that avalanche?"

He rose to his feet, making her feel insignificant by his towering height. "I want you to use some sense, to stay away from dangerous situations like that. That cornice . . ."

"I didn't know the cornice would break! I didn't even know it was a cornice!"

"Then you had no business going out there!"

She couldn't allow him to go on. "Look, I may be partly guilty, but I don't deserve all the blame!" Her voice was rising, but she could not control it. "Linc . . ."

"You didn't follow in Linc's tracks. He veered away from the danger point. He told me all about it, how you went off on your own. You're a stubborn . . ."

Jennifer's hands balled into fists. "I took a shortcut! I was so tired. . . . I know I was foolish, but Linc was foolish to take me beyond my ability. I'll share the punishment, but I won't take all of it." Now she was shouting.

"Who said you had to take all of it?" Dominic's jaw firmed; his eyes bored into her as if to nail her to the wall behind her.

"Why . . . I . . . you . . ."

"Linc's got the broken leg. Knocks him out for the rest of the season. You think that isn't punishment for a guy who earns his living on skis?"

He swung away from her, turned to face the window behind his desk. Standing with his feet widespread and his hands clasped behind his back, he said without looking around at her, "Now, for heaven's sake, Jennifer, go back to your room and rest. Your face tells me you need it. You're not to set foot outside your room until tomorrow, and not outside the lodge until the following day. Understand? I'll have your meals sent to your room."

He turned back to his desk, and picking up a sheaf of papers began to study the one on top, as if she had already left the room and he had forgotten her.

When she had started to turn away and leave, he brought her back with his words, clipped and cold, "Here's your hat."

Jennifer swung around and saw that he held out the pink hat to her. "No thank you," she said politely. "I don't want it."

"Oh?" Both his eyebrows shot up on his forehead.

"I never want to see that hat again," she said. She snatched the hat, flung it into the wastebasket, and walked out.

But it wasn't the hat, it was Dominic Martin who had sent her temper flaring again. In a way she didn't quite understand, he had made the hat a part of the challenge between them.

And he had left no doubt in Jennifer's mind that he hated her more than ever for what he considered her stupidity.

And he even had the nerve to tell me I look a mess! she reminded herself, as she made her way wearily back to her room.

She spent a good part of the day fuming at Dominic Martin. Lying in bed, alternating between dream-troubled sleep and wakeful staring at the walls of her room, she damned him. As he had promised, Dominic had meals sent to her room, but Jennifer was too miserable to do more than pick at the food.

Late that afternoon, however, she grew tired of staring at the four walls of her room. She blamed Dominic unmercifully for ordering her to stay inside. After shampooing her hair, however, she felt better. She could think more logically.

She considered herself no longer an employee at Rainbow Lodge. After all, she had resigned from her job as Activities Coordinator. She told herself she didn't care what Dominic did about replacing her, but a gnawing curiosity grew within her. What was going on outside the closed door of her room?

On the second day after her experience in the avalanche, Jennifer awoke feeling refreshed and invigorated. She could not wait to leave the monotony of her room. She dressed in her favorite plaid slacks, and slipped on her red sweater.

As she brushed her hair she peered critically into the

mirror. Her color had returned as had the sheen to her hair. She would show Dominic Martin that she no longer looked a mess.

When at last she was ready, she hurried out into the lounge. It was deserted, but through the window Jennifer could see the bright figures dotting the slopes. It was plain to see that Dominic no longer needed her as Activities Coordinator. Everything was running smoothly without her.

The door to Dominic's office was closed, and not even Cassie was at her post at the reception counter. Jennifer shut her mind to the possibilities of the two somewhere together.

She went to the dining room and loaded her tray from the warming table. Everything smelled delicious this morning, from coffee in the big urn to the crisp bacon kept hot on its platter. She enjoyed a big breakfast.

While she ate she made a decision. Since she was a paying guest here now, she might as well get full measure of the enjoyment the Rainbow had to offer. She would stay until her money ran out. She told herself that Dominic had nothing whatsoever to do with her reluctance to leave. She cared nothing for the fact that once she left the Rainbow she would never see him again.

He's going to marry Cassie, she reminded herself firmly. *And the sooner I cut loose from him the better it will be.*

But she could enjoy a few more days of skiing, another part of her persisted.

She might as well start today. She finished her breakfast, and put her empty dishes into the bin left for that purpose. Then she hurried back to her room for her outdoor clothing. Although Dominic had ordered one more day of staying indoors for her, he wasn't around to enforce his edict. He had underestimated Jennifer's recuperative powers, she told herself.

But when she went to her closet, she could not find her green ski outfit. She searched her room, looking in unlikely places such as under the bed as well as likely places. The green outfit was simply not there, and it was too cold and windy to ski in lighter clothing.

Jennifer stood in the middle of the room, frowning. Then she remembered that she had left the green outfit in Dominic's room and he had obviously neglected to return it. So that was the way Dominic had of making sure she obeyed his orders! Aloud, she said, "Of all the underhanded, unreasonable, arrogant . . ." Anger thickened her tongue and blunted her thinking so that she had no more names to call him.

She spent the remainder of the day indoors, but she did not see Dominic. From outside came the howling and excited yelping of his dogs, and she guessed that he spent much of the time with them.

It seemed as if every wall had eyes to watch that she did not try to venture out into the snow, and Jennifer felt an ugly knot of suspicion tighten within her whenever one of the ski instructors passed her with a friendly wave or a greeting. Maybe he had turned them into spies for him, to make certain she did not borrow a jacket and go outside. She sighed. All because of Dominic, she was growing bitter and suspicious.

The new guests were eager to make the most of the opportunity to ski. The lounge was virtually deserted, and Jennifer roamed it restlessly.

That evening when everyone gathered around the fire, they formed enthusiastic small groups to relive the excitement of their day's experiences in the snow. Jennifer felt useless, left out and lonely.

When she discovered a group planning a cross-country outing the next day, she asked to join. One of the ski instructors was to lead the expedition. He gave her a raised eyebrow look. "You up to that much activity yet, Jennifer?"

"Of course," she said stoutly. "It's like when you get thrown by a horse. You need to ride again as soon as possible so you don't build up a fear."

He agreed, but reluctantly, and she signed up for the party. For the first time in days her spirits lifted.

That night Jennifer discovered that her green ski outfit had been returned, mended and freshened, brushed free of the caked mud. She laughed wryly. It was neat and serviceable, but no longer would she be mistaken for a nonskier while wearing it. It looked well-used.

Who had thought to have it repaired? She could not believe Dominic was capable of such consideration.

When she slept, she dreamed of Dominic, his hair gilded by the winter sun, driving his dogs through the white wilderness.

She awoke early that morning, excitement racing through her as she anticipated the skiing excursion.

This time, she thought, *I'll follow so faithfully in the ski tracks it'll look as if only one skier's been there.*

After breakfast she joined the others, half a dozen people of various ages, and the ski instructor, at the base of the poma lift.

Spirits were high, and there was much laughter

among the group of people dressed in brightly colored ski clothing. Jennifer felt happier than she had felt for days.

Because most of the skiers in the party lacked expertise, the instructor had chosen an easy trail. The skiers followed single file, traversing the slope with their rhythmic kick-glide step, digging one pole and then the other into the snow to help propel them along.

The trail began to climb, and the skiers had to struggle harder. Some of them lagged behind and the line became ragged and uneven.

At first Jennifer was able to keep up easily with the skier ahead of her, but soon she discovered that one day of rest, followed by another of confinement in the lodge, had not completely restored her. The space between her and the skier ahead grew longer.

In the middle of the morning she had to call out, asking for a rest stop. The trail had grown steeper, and exhaustion had turned Jennifer's legs to rubber.

The ski instructor followed the rule laid down by Dominic for all his ski tours. Anyone's request for a rest halt must be honored by the entire group. As was usual, the stop brought out the fact that others were beginning to tire also.

There was no dry place where the skiers could sit, for every stump, every log, every boulder was covered with snow, but Jennifer found that just standing still, with a little support from her ski poles, gave her some rest.

The instructor handed out portions of trail mix, a combination of nuts, dried fruits, seeds and coconut. While Jennifer munched hers, the sound of Dominic's dogs' yelps cut through the clear air. Jennifer turned her back on the sound as if turning away could shut from her thoughts the picture of Dominic and his dogs. She was sure Cassie must be with him, and she tried to tell herself that Cassie's rightful place was by Dominic's side. After all, she was engaged to him. But the thought was like a fish bone lodged in her throat. It seemed to cut off her breath and choke her.

Shortly afterward, they started on again, but, for Jennifer, the joy had gone from the experience.

A half hour later, the dogsled's path intersected theirs, and Jennifer found herself face to face with Dominic Martin himself. Cassie, she noted, was not riding in the sled, nor anywhere to be seen.

For some reason Dominic's attention was directed toward her. The ski instructor halted the line of skiers at his signal. He left his sled and came straight over to her, his boots sinking deep into the snow with every step.

"What are you doing out here skiing?" he demanded, scowling at her.

Jennifer faced him with her chin thrust out. "I'm a paying guest now, I'm entitled to ski when I choose."

"It's too soon. You're not up to it."

"I've come this far. I can do all right the rest of the way too." She hoped her voice didn't betray the sudden lack of confidence she felt. She refused to admit to Dominic Martin that she was tired.

"Take off your skis and get into the sled," he said, jerking his head toward where the team of dogs waited impatiently, yelping and restlessly tugging at their harness.

Jennifer was going to refuse, but the other skiers shouted encouragement.

"Hey, Jennifer!" someone called out. "You're not going to turn down a chance to ride in a dogsled, are you?"

"I'll go in your place, Jennifer. Gladly," another shouted.

Jennifer did not want to cause a scene.

With a resigned shrug of her shoulders she bent down to unfasten the bindings of her skis.

After she had removed her skis, she had expected to make her own way through the snow, but Dominic lifted her easily and carried her over to set her down among the blankets. Bending to tuck the blankets around her, he whispered, "Do you expect my dogs and me to spend the rest of our lives rescuing you?"

Jennifer's face was on fire as she replied haughtily, "You saved my life before and I'm grateful, but this time I neither asked nor needed to be rescued."

The party of skiers had moved on, and Dominic turned away to pick up her skis from the snow. His voice came back to her as he said, "Maybe you didn't need rescuing yet, but it wouldn't be long before you'd have become a drag on that party. That could endanger you and all the rest of them. You don't realize what an ordeal you've been through."

He slapped the two skis together, knocking snow from them. As Jennifer heard the resounding *clack*, she thought, *He'd like to be hitting me instead of the skis*.

Without further comment Dominic stowed her skis in a rack built onto the sled, then grasping the extension of the sled's back, he adjusted the direction in which it was headed. "Go!" he shouted to the dogs. They scarcely needed the command to release their boundless energy. The sled jerked as Dominic helped unstick the runners for the dogs to race over the snowy mountainside. While Jennifer grasped the sled's sides to help maintain her balance, Dominic ran alongside or sometimes behind it. Sometimes he leaped onto the runners to help guide the sled.

This was the first time Jennifer had been able to enjoy riding behind the dogs. They sped through a white landscape broken only by the black-green silhouettes of evergreens, their yelps echoing wild music in the woodland silence. Dominic was intent on guiding the sled, easing it around great white-coated boulders and the fallen trunks of mighty trees. Though she wanted to be angry at him for his high-handed treatment of her, she could not help admiring the grace and skill with which he drove his dogs; they moved as a single unit over the crystal country. He seemed to be completely unaware of the girl beside him, while she was storing up every detail about him—his flaming hair, the rugged line of his jaw, the flaring nostrils and piercing blue eyes now blazing with excitement.

She turned away, afraid he would see the love she knew her face must reveal. *Why can't I stop loving you, Dominic Martin,* she thought.

In time she began to realize that they were climbing, whereas the lodge lay below them.

She called out, "Where are we going, Dominic?"

Perhaps he did not hear her. Or perhaps he was too busy handling the dogs to answer. In any case, there was no reply, and Jennifer resigned herself to waiting.

At last they came to a small cabin built of native stone. Jennifer had never seen it before, and she knew they were far from any of the Rainbow's downhill slopes. The snow around the hut drifted high around the plank door. There was no column of smoke rising from the chimney. The cabin appeared to be deserted.

Dominic brought the dogs to a halt, tying their traces to a tall post beside the doorway.

"What are we doing here?" Jennifer asked.

"It's a shelter for hikers and skiers," he said. "The dogs need a rest, even though they'll deny it if you give them a chance. And I need to get a few matters straightened out with you."

What will happen if I agree to go into the cabin with him? Jennifer asked herself, and found desire warring with her judgment.

He made his way through the deep snow to the cabin's door. Reaching up, he took from high on the outer wall a shovel Jennifer had not noticed. With powerful thrusts, he dug the shovel into the snow and cleared away the snow for the door to swing open.

Replacing the shovel on its hook, he turned to her. "Come on in," he said. "We'll light a fire."

From the sled, she peered into the dark cabin. A wad of cotton seemed to fill her throat and mouth. If I stay in the sled, she reasoned, neither of us can get into trouble. She tried to think of Cassie and her duty to the girl.

Dominic stared at her, frowning. When it appeared certain that she would not leave the sled of her own free will, he shrugged and stalked back through the deep snow until he stood beside the sled. "I'm not going to rape you. I just want us to talk things out." Bending over, he scooped Jennifer and the blankets that wrapped her into his arms, and carried her across the snow and into the cabin.

Just to talk things out, he had said. But Jennifer knew how dangerous talking could be. She trembled in his arms. The trembling increased as Dominic kicked the cabin's door closed behind them.

Chapter Twelve

Though she would have denied it, Jennifer had enjoyed
the pleasant sensation of being carried over the threshold and into the little mountain cabin by Dominic. It
was like the traditional bridegroom carrying his bride
over the threshold and into their new home.

But the smile died quickly on her lips, for she wasn't
his bride. She never would be. Cassie had already been
chosen for that role.

With a sigh that she hoped was not audible, Jennifer
rested her head against the strength of his shoulder for
the briefest of moments before Dominic set her on her
feet. He crossed to the woodbox beside the open
fireplace.

The interior of the hut was dark after the bright glare
of the snow outside. Jennifer brushed her hair back

from her face and stood blinking her eyes in an effort to bring everything into focus. She was still shaking. There was no sound from outside except for an occasional howl from one of the dogs that seemed only to emphasize the vast emptiness of the wilderness. What temptation would Dominic lead her into? How could she control her responses to this man she so hopelessly loved?

As her eyes adjusted, the room emerged from the darkness. Two small windows had been built into facing walls of the cabin, flanking the fireplace. They were covered with plastic that must originally have been clear but now was scratched and scarred into semi-opacity. They let in only a small amount of light. By it Jennifer watched Dominic for a moment as he lifted logs from the woodbox and laid them carefully on the iron fire grate.

The room had the damp chill of an unoccupied building, although a faint scent of pine mingling with the odor of smoke from countless fires told of its history.

Folding her arms close around her body to shut out the cold, Jennifer turned to look around the room.

Bed frames had been stacked, like bunk beds, against the windowless wall, and more of these cots stood single decked under the windows. The frames were unlike any she had seen before, and she bent to examine one of them. It was obviously hand fashioned, with posts of slender trunks from young pine trees, partially stripped of their bark. She sniffed. It was from these posts that the fresh scent of pine came to perfume the room's air.

Instead of springs, each of the beds boasted a network of interwoven leather straps. When Jennifer eased herself down to sit on one of them, there was the creak of leather stretching against leather as it gave in much the same way a spring mattress would have done.

Dominic, hunched over his feet before the fireplace, had turned to observe her. Leaning back on his heels he grinned at her. "An ingenious idea, isn't it? The four-legged little people of the woods would have made mincemeat long ago of a stuffed mattress. Hikers bring their own blankets or sleeping bags."

"You mean . . . people actually stay here?"

He laughed. "Would you prefer to spend the night out in the snow?" A wave of his hand illustrated.

Jennifer swallowed back a gasp. "I'm not . . . We aren't . . ." She drew herself up. "I will not stay here with you, Dominic Martin!" She did not add, *I don't trust you. I don't trust myself.*

"Who asked you to spend the night? I only meant if you were a skier caught out in a storm, or a hiker." With quick, jerky motions, he turned back to lighting the fire, giving her no opportunity to reply.

Jennifer could not think of an answer that was scathing enough to express her humiliation and the resulting anger. Dominic was forever baiting a trap, then watching her blunder into it, as she had done now.

But had he been the one to set the trap, another part of her prodded. Wasn't it her own assumption that had tripped her? Embarrassed, she returned to her scrutiny of the cabin's interior.

The floor consisted of flat, slatelike stones laid edge to edge in a haphazard pattern. Some of the built-in shelves were open, and she saw that they were well stocked with canned soups and meats, jars of beans, rice and spaghetti. Food to help hungry, outdoors people last out any storm.

She was thankful that the sun was shining this day, and that they would return before dark.

The fire was taking hold now, blue and orange flames curling up between and around the logs. Its warmth had already taken the edge from the chill of the room.

Dominic stood up. His jacket was unzipped, and Jennifer unzipped hers, but she did not remove hers yet as he did before he came to sit on the cot beside her.

"No cushions," he said. "Because of the little four-footed people."

The distinctive scent of him, the scent that reminded her of lemon and sandalwood and male strength and the out-of-doors, came to tantalize her. His very nearness was a danger to her. She rose to her feet, too quickly perhaps, for he grinned at her.

"The hearth's as comfortable and there's more warmth down there near the fire," she said. Even to herself it sounded like a lame excuse, but she did not care.

She went to sit down on the hearth, knees bent and her arms wrapped around them, as she watched the dancing flames.

Quickly she realized the heat was too much even though her parka hung open. Without getting up, she began to squirm out of it.

Dominic rose and came to help her out of the sleeves, then he sat down cross-legged beside her.

She stiffened involuntarily. She had moved away

from him deliberately. Now by coming to sit close to her he had defeated her purpose. This was only slightly less dangerous than sitting together on the bed. Jennifer stared into the fire, neither speaking nor looking at him.

A full half minute stretched out in which she heard no sound except the faint sigh of his breathing and the roar and crackle of the fire as flames leaped up the chimney. She did not trust herself to glance at Dominic, and her tongue seemed as paralyzed as her mind.

Then abruptly, he spoke. "Jennifer," he said, and she braced herself for whatever would come next. "I know you're not completely indifferent to me. You've shown by your actions that I can stir you in the same way you stir me. But suddenly I feel you've gathered all your strength, all your forces, to fight against me. You're determined to shut me out of your thoughts, maybe even out of your life. Is it because you're in love with Linc?"

She swung around to face him, widening her eyes in her very real astonishment. "In love with Linc? Me? You must be crazy! I could never be in love with Linc. How could you ever think that?"

He grinned, but did not meet her gaze, only shrugging his massive shoulders. "Well, he gave you that pink hat, and Cassie said . . ."

So he thought the hat and Linc were important to her. And . . . "Cassie! How can you believe all the stupid lies . . . ?" Jennifer broke off as she remembered that Cassie was the one Dominic would marry.

Now he turned back to fix her with his stare. For long moments she was held by the force of his sapphire eyes. *That does it,* she thought. *Now I've made him hate me*

178

worse than ever. Now he knows what I think of Cassie, his Cassie. Jennifer seemed to shrivel inside.

At last Dominic said, his voice quiet, "You don't like Cassie, do you, Jennifer?"

Jennifer thought, *I don't think Cassie is worthy of so much as one of your smiles, let alone your love!*

But of course she could not say that. She remained silent.

"You don't understand Cassie. Did you know she was the one who mended your ski clothes?"

"Cassie! But I thought . . . I thought you . . ."

"I hinted it might be wise. Cassie agreed. Perhaps I should tell you about Cassie. Then maybe you'll understand."

Jennifer longed to say, *Already I understand too much about Cassie.* But that would only make him think she was jealous.

And I am jealous, she admitted ruefully to herself. But it was too late now for jealousy. It would do her no good and would not change Cassie.

Dominic interrupted her thoughts. Jennifer came alert to hear only part of his sentence, ". . . ran away from her husband and baby."

Instantly her attention was fastened onto him. "Husband . . . baby . . . Cassie?"

Dominic nodded. "She was very young when she married and had had no chance to enjoy her youth before settling down to responsibilities. She wasn't strong enough to handle them."

He went on to explain that the husband wanted her back, and had appealed to Dominic to be the mediator between them. "Cassie and I've had some very serious talks. I think she's about ready to return. She misses her baby, and she's had her fling here at the Rainbow. She's talking more and more about her husband. He's a nice guy."

Jennifer shook her head incredulously. "Then why did she tell me she was engaged to you?" The words burst from her without her direction.

"Cassie said she was engaged to me?"

Jennifer explained about the ring Cassie had said she and Dominic were going to select.

He laughed, the sound untroubled. "If that isn't just like Cassie!"

"I don't see anything funny about lying!"

Dominic turned toward Jennifer, catching both her hands in his. She longed to fight against him, but she allowed her hands to remain in his.

"Jennifer, you must understand how little inner security Cassie has. She trusts me to help her, and I'm afraid her fear of losing my help makes her possessive of me."

"So possessive she brags that you love her." Jennifer knew there was bitterness in her own words, but she could not keep from saying them.

"But I do," Dominic replied, "but not in the way you think. Or she claims. And I hope that I have been able to help her over a rough time. But now it's time for her to stand on her own two feet, and I mean to see that she does just that. I've asked her husband to come up to the Rainbow to spend a few days getting reacquainted in a relaxed environment. I hope she'll return with him."

Now Jennifer felt the sting of compunction. She lowered her eyes to avoid meeting his frank blue gaze. "I . . . I guess I've been too hasty in condemning Cassie. After all, if it hadn't been for her, you wouldn't have known Linc and I were caught in the avalanche. I'm really grateful to her."

"You can be helpful to her too, Jennifer. Cassie needs friends. Be one."

She made an attempt to smile as she looked at him. "I'll try, Dominic."

"That would help me too, Jennifer," he said thoughtfully. "It's hard being all alone, trying to keep everybody happy, especially when we're forced to stay inside the lodge during a storm."

He went on to talk about his problems in running the ski resort by himself. "Many times I have to be a father to those kids who work for me, and a mother too." He laughed. "I make a pretty poor mother, but . . . well . . ." He shrugged. "I need a partner to help me run the lodge and to help me run my life." He was staring into the fire, all traces of humor gone from his face.

"And Cassie isn't the one to fill that spot after all?"

"Cassie? Of course not. She was never even a candidate. Cassie's got potential, but that guy she's already married to is right for her, and I hope I've convinced her of that. No, it could never be Cassie and me, but . . ."

Jennifer waited for him to go on. And waited. The fire crackled and a log resettled itself, sending up a shower of sparks that illuminated the rugged profile of Dominic Martin. He sat so close beside her on the hearth yet so far away from her heart.

And still he said nothing.

Unable to bear the suspense, Jennifer said, "But you do have someone in mind? Someone else?"

He was staring into the fire when he answered, and

there was a gentleness in the single word he spoke. "Yes."

Again the silence closed around them, with only the crackle of the flames to break it.

At last Jennifer rose to her feet. "I think we should get started back." Perhaps he didn't want to talk about this girl.

Still staring into the fire, Dominic Martin said, "Yes, I suppose we might as well."

Jennifer thought she had never heard such weariness, such discouragement as were contained in those words.

Apparently the girl did not return his love. *What a fool she must be,* Jennifer thought. Dominic was everything a girl could want. Any girl who did not realize that was foolish—or blind! She turned away so that he could not see the anguish of her face.

Who was this unknown girl who had won the coveted prize of Dominic Martin's love?

She felt she had to get out of this lonely cabin fast before she betrayed herself by showing her love for Dominic who was in love with someone else. She picked up her parka and eased her arms into it. Zipping it up determinedly, she crossed to the door.

Before opening it, she glanced back over her shoulder at Dominic. Without moving from his position he was watching her.

"We really must get back, Dominic," she said.

He sighed heavily and rose to his feet. "The fire's going nicely. It'll soon have this place as cozy as your own room. A shame to leave it."

Jennifer turned away. "There's no point in staying," she said. She thought, *What's the point of staying here since he has already admitted he is in love with someone else.*

She reached for the door's handle.

Before she could open the door, the dogs set up a howling and yelping that brought Dominic instantly to Jennifer's side. He reached beyond her to grasp the door's latch and swing the door open.

A shower of snowflakes blew in on an icy gust of wind.

"Oh, no!" Dominic cried. "Another blizzard!"

Jennifer was shocked into speechlessness. Where was the sunshine that had brightened their journey to this remote spot?

At last she managed to say, "It can't be!"

His laugh was short. "Oh, but it can. It is." He slammed the door closed and stood with his hand still on the latch. "Sudden, unexpected storms come up now and then. We have to accept them. That's why this place is kept stocked." For a moment he looked down at her, then he said, "You know what this means, don't you?"

It meant they were trapped here, unable to leave the tiny cabin. Jennifer looked up at him without saying anything. The blood drained from her face. She could not form the words to answer his question.

Dominic spoke for her, saying what she already knew was true. "We can't travel in this storm. I wouldn't ask the dogs to attempt it. We'd be lost before we'd gone a mile. We'll have to wait out the storm here."

Panic clutched at Jennifer. It could have been panic about the physical danger, or it could have been panic for what might happen between them, what she would not be strong enough to prevent happening. Perhaps it was both, and the vague image of the other girl, the girl who was lucky enough to have Dominic's love, seemed to materialize into a physical presence there in the room with them.

Dominic must have seen the panic in her face, for he said, "We'll be safe, even comfortable. There's plenty of dry wood, a good supply of food, and we've brought blankets. I'll go out now and settle the dogs in the lean-to in back."

The door opened and closed behind him, and Jennifer was left alone with only a melting puddle of snowy slush beside the closed door to show that it had been open.

The draft had sucked a puff of smoke from the fire out into the room, and with its scent Jennifer thought she caught the lingering hint of his aftershave.

"Oh, Dominic," she whispered. "What can I do to protect myself from the power you have over me?"

In an effort to distract her thoughts, she used the time of Dominic's absence to mop up the melting snow on the floor. Then she investigated the store of supplies in the cabin. In a closed cabinet she found a kettle that was meant for use over an open fire. But there was no hook in the fireplace from which to hang it. *Perhaps Dominic would have an idea,* she thought, and went on to see what food might be suitable for their next meal.

One shelf contained nothing but canned dog food, and Jennifer stared at it. Dominic must come often to this cabin. Had he brought the girl he loved here? Did the two of them spend days here together? Jennifer's eyes were drawn to the bed frames as if by a magnet. Each of the beds had been designed for one person alone, yet they could adequately accommodate two, especially on a cold night. . . .

When Dominic returned, the two of them were kept occupied for a time shaking snow from his jacket, placing his gloves where they would dry without scorching, and mopping up the snow that inevitably blew in with each opening of the door.

The dogs were settled, he told her; he had fed them some of the meat he always carried in the sled. "It's frozen, of course, but their teeth can handle that, and I save the canned stuff to use only as a last resort."

When these tasks had been completed, an awkward silence grew between them. Jennifer found that the intimacy of their circumstances left her tongue-tied and stiff. Perhaps it was the same with Dominic, for he seemed as much at a loss for words as she.

At last she suggested they start preparing their meal. He appeared grateful for the suggestion.

Dominic's solution to the problem of cooking over the open fire was simple. By now the fire had built up a good bed of coals, and with the poker he raked some of them to one side, spread them out, and set the pot directly into them.

They emptied several cans of meat and vegetables into the pot, added melted snow and rice. Covering the pot with its own lid, Dominic scooped up more coals with the fireplace shovel and sprinkled them on top of the lid. "That'll cook it nicely," he said.

Throughout all this activity, few words had been exchanged between them, and these had to do with nothing except the chores they performed.

But once the stew was cooking over the fire, there was nothing to talk about. For a time Jennifer and

Dominic sat side by side on the stone hearth in silence. Jennifer's knees had been drawn up and she hugged them with her arms while Dominic sat cross-legged, staring into the glowing fire.

At last Jennifer said, "How long do you expect this storm to last?"

He did not look at her as he answered, "Hard to say. It could be over by tomorrow morning, or it could last a week."

She was watching him, and the flickering glow from the fire made the strong line of his jaw gleam in its light, while shadows filled the hollows below his high cheekbones. In the ruddy firelight, his profile might have been a bas-relief study in copper. Jennifer's heart turned over.

"A week," she repeated, and sighed. "I can believe we won't suffer discomfort. But what will we do with all that time?"

He did not look at her still, but a wry smile curved the corners of his mouth.

Uneasiness troubled Jennifer, and she said, "I hope she won't suspect the worst of us."

Now he did turn to look at her. "She? Who?"

"Your girl."

"What girl?"

"The girl you said you're in love with. I hope she won't get the wrong idea about what we're doing out here alone together."

Again the smile twisted his mouth. Turning his head to stare into the fire again, he said softly, "I don't see how she could, since she's right here."

Jennifer glanced surreptitiously around as if she really expected to see this girl watching over Dominic.

Slowly realization dawned.

"Dominic!" she cried. "You don't mean . . . You can't mean . . . *I'm* the one?"

"Who else?"

Her arms reached out to him. "I've loved you so long. . . ."

He stared at her. "You? You've a very strange way of showing it."

"I didn't think. . . . I can't believe. . . ."

Now his hands reached, then drew back, and he frowned. "You said you wouldn't work for me. Don't you like living at the Rainbow?"

Jennifer laughed uncertainly. "Of course I do. I love it, maybe as much as you do. But working for you. . . ."

"How about working *with* me then?"

"I'd like that. . . ." He pulled her close. As she settled into the curve of his shoulder, she thought, *How can I tell him I don't want to settle for anything less than marriage?* It felt so right to snuggle close to him.

"You don't sound very sure," he said, then thrusting her away, he searched her face. "How can I convince you, sitting here on this blasted hard stone?" He pulled her to her feet as he rose. When they were standing he gathered her close again into his arms.

She responded to his kiss, molding herself against him. Again she felt passion rising in him that matched the passion rising from deep within herself.

She must control herself. She had to tell him that she was not interested in a transient relationship no matter how much she loved him.

It was Dominic who broke away. He said, "To think of all the time we've wasted. Come over here, Jennifer.

I've a very good idea of how we can spend our time while we're snowed in here, and I hope it's a long storm."

"No, Dominic!" she cried. "I can't . . . I won't . . . Not without marriage!"

"Without . . . What did you think I meant? What kind of a man do you think I am?" A dangerous light came into his eyes. Jennifer decided that this was not a question that she wished to answer.

"The only man for me," she murmured, lifting her lips for the sweet fire of his kiss.

Silhouette *Romance*

THE NEW NAME IN LOVE STORIES

Six new titles every month bring you the best in romance.
Set all over the world, exciting and brand new stories about
people falling in love:

Silhouette Romance

THE NEW NAME IN LOVE STORIES

Silhouette *Romance*

THE NEW NAME IN LOVE STORIES

*All these books are available at your local bookshop or
newsagent, or can be ordered direct from the publisher. Just
tick the titles you want and fill in the form below.*

Prices and availability subject to change without notice.

———————————————————————

SILHOUETTE BOOKS, P.O. Box 11, Falmouth, Cornwall.

Please send cheque or postal order, and allow the following for
postage and packing:

U.K. — 40p for one book, plus 18p for the second book, and
13p for each additional book ordered, up to £1.49 maximum.

B.F.P.O. and EIRE — 40p for the first book, 18p for the
second book, and 13p per copy for the next 7 books, 7p per
book thereafter.

OTHER OVERSEAS CUSTOMERS — 60p for the first book
plus 18p per copy for each additional book.

Name ....

Address...

....

Silhouette *Romance*

EXCITING MEN,
EXCITING PLACES, HAPPY ENDINGS . . .

Contemporary romances for today's women

If there's room in your life for a little more romance,
SILHOUETTE ROMANCES are for you.

And you won't want to miss a single one so start
your collection now.

Each month, six very special love stories will be yours
from SILHOUETTE.

Look for them wherever books are sold
or order from the coupon below.